Despera

Desperately Seeking
Julio

MARUJA TORRES

★ ★

TRANSLATED BY ANN WRIGHT

Fourth Estate · *London*

First published in Spain in 1986 by Editorial Anagrama
First published in Great Britain in 1991 by
Fourth Estate Limited
289 Westbourne Grove
London W11 2QA

A catalogue record for this book is available from the British Library

ISBN 1-872180-79-5

Typeset by York House Typographic Ltd, London
Printed in Great Britain by Biddles Ltd., Guildford

Contents

★ ★

Prologue

★ ★

The author wishes to point out that this novel, or whatever it is, is simply a product of her feverish imagination (for lack of anything else) and that all the characters are invented. In those cases where the names used might vaguely remind the reader of someone slightly famous, the author feels bound to say she is paying a simple, plain, heartfelt tribute, not to real people but to the fantasy – or perhaps the myth – that the mere image of their names conjures up.

The idol, in his golden splendour

★ ★

A hundred and twenty kilos of muscular blond angel were snoozing in a deck-chair by the door of 1100 Bel Air Place, on his knees a walkie-talkie connected to the main gate of the plush residential suburb. Beyond the brief but impenetrable garden, the clear bright-blue kidney of a swimming-pool hung like a jewel in the Hollywood hills.

Suddenly, out of the translucent waters, emerged an exceptionally good-looking male face.

'O magic pool,' said Julio Iglesias, 'who's the greatest singer in the world?'

'Frank Sinatra,' replied the pool ominously.

A murmur of protest ran round the terrace, from where a group of the superstar's friends, colleagues and family was surveying the scene.

The idol's faithful secretary was just about to rush up and feed him a strawberry bonbon, but Julio, who had eyes in the back of his head, stopped him in his tracks with a princely gesture.

'Wait,' he ordered, 'I want to ask it something else.' He took a deep breath and asked, 'O magic pool, what other singer nearly died in an unfortunate accident that changed the course of his life by forcing him to give up a brilliant career as goalie for Real Madrid? What other singer was deserted by his wife? What other singer's father was kidnapped by ETA?'

The pool was silent, humiliated.

I

'You see?' crowed Julio, jubilant. 'I'm the greatest.'

Murmurs of assent from the chorus. Tony Rennis began to sing softly, jangling his medallions, bracelets, rings and solid gold teeth as he did. *'Sei grande, grande, grande, solamente tu . . .'*

'Where has Alfredo got to?'

'He's in the Amphitheatre checking everything for your opening night.'

'Good. It has to be perfect.'

You could see he was pleased. He let his body be dried gently and asked the French housekeeper to lay his white linen trousers, Italian shoes and red jacket.

'I'm going to be a hit,' he said to himself, although audibly.

His father, who'd been watching him in silence, lost in a trance of supreme happiness, suddenly hung his bag on the branch of a dwarf palm and, his hands free, began to clap.

'If they don't make you a roving ambassador for Spain after this, there's no justice in the world.'

Julio made a tiny gesture of modesty, waving the idea aside. 'How am I doing in *Billboard?*'

'Brilliant,' replied his press secretary. 'On top.'

'Yes, but with Willie Nelson. I want to be up there alone.'

A shadow of anxiety crossed his face fleetingly. The others flinched, terrified. They couldn't allow the singer a fit of depression only hours before his show in the Los Angeles Amphitheatre.

A quick-witted aide opened a cupboard and brought out one of the exquisitely beautiful blondes kept for such occasions. He took aim, pushed her forward, and the girl landed in the space formed by Julio's left arm.

'Get her out of here,' said the singer, laconically. 'And leave me alone. I need to concentrate.'

When the others had gone, he went back to the pool.

'O magic pool . . .'

It didn't let him finish.

'I said Frank Sinatra, for Christ's sake.'

Julio was silent, his eyes fixed on the city he had sworn to take by storm, which lay spread out at his feet.

Big changes in the life of Encarna Alférez

★ ★

Encarna Alférez took two decisions as she applied dark green mascara (to make her look mysterious) in the toilet of the magazine *Rumour*. One: have her hair cut at Llongueras Unisex in a daring short-back-and-sides and aggressive fringe. Two: change her name.

That is, be A Modern Woman.

'Encarna!' Tender Titi's voice bellowed through the door.

She pursed her lips. From now on she would be Diana Dial, intrepid reporter, expert on Life.

She came out a couple of minutes later, banging the door. 'What's wrong?'

Titi looked at her quizzically. 'What have you put on our eyes? You look like Richard Harris in *A Man Called Horse*.'

'Fucking poofta!'

Titi, who was in charge of the archives, had been caught more than once having a quick wank with El Puma's dossier open on his lap. El Puma was his idol, hence the bad blood between him and Encarna, a Julio Iglesias fan.

'Viceversa wants you. He's in a foul mood.'

She crossed the editorial office amid silence. Whenever the boss summoned her, her colleagues first pondered the reason, and then, with a lack of urgency that showed why they worked on *Rumour* and not on the *Washington Post*, speculated.

3

'He's going to fire her.'

'Don't be silly. They've got a thing going.'

Diana Dial walked contemptuously through their midst, head held high. So high that she banged into at least three drawers that some dimwit had left open.

She knocked on Viceversa's door.

'I'm very busy,' said a voice. 'So come in.'

They called the boss Viceversa because he was always contradicting himself. Like all bosses in fact. Rather than handsome, Encarna found him very interesting. His office was so big that Ray Conniff, his orchestra and his chorus could have performed quite comfortably in it.

'Yes?'

Encarna was nervous, because Viceversa always looked at her tits before he looked at her eyes. She didn't know that her tits reminded him of his mother, so she was always afraid one of her buttons was undone, or her padded bra strap had slipped and, right there under Viceversa's snout, her tits were all wonky.

'I've been thinking about your future. What did you do yesterday?'

'I started on next week's serial. You know, the one about White Russians.'

'Ah, yes,' Viceversa said vaguely. 'Fancy taking a trip?'

Encarna blushed. At last, just like in Chapter Twelve of her third serial for *Rumour*! The boss was going to suggest They Have An Affair.

'I'm giving you *carte blanche* to follow Julio Iglesias on his tour of the States. He's going to be a hit in the US and *Rumour* has to be there. You're ideal for the job. You know more about Julio than anyone here.'

'Yes, I do!' exclaimed Diana Dial, ecstatic. 'I had dinner with him once, and another time he took my hand during a rehearsal.'

'Get going, then. And make us proud of you.'

She left the office with her face transformed. The others nudged one another.

'What's wrong with her?' asked the receptionist.

'Maybe she's unpredictable,' said Titi.

4

Encarna sat down at her typewriter to work on the new chapter of her serial. But her heart wasn't in it, and her mind had taken flight. All the same, she tapped away quickly, spurred on by habit:

'WHAT WOULD HAVE BECOME OF SONIA, ALONE AT THAT TRAIN STATION IN THE MIDDLE OF THE SNOWY STEPPES, IF AT THAT VERY MOMENT A COSSACK, WHOSE FIERY EYES DEVOURED HER AS IF HE WANTED TO UNDRESS HER AND MAKE HER HIS RIGHT THERE AND THEN, HADN'T COME UP AND KISSED HER PASSIONATELY?'

'Psst, psst.'

Ignacio Clavé (or Saladino when he signed *Rumour*'s horoscope page) was making signs at her from his desk nearby.

'Is it true they're sending you to Miami?'

'To Los Angeles first,' said Encarna, precisely. 'Why?'

'Will you see him?'

'Who?'

'Julio.'

She nodded, then typed on:

'AS HE TORE AT HER SILK PETTICOATS, SHE FELT HER BREATH QUICKEN.'

'I have something for him.'

'What?'

'I'll tell you tonight if you come round.'

She looked at him suspiciously. The last time Ignacio Clavé had invited her round, on the pretext of doing her astrological chart, he ended up trying to rape her during the TV news.

'Please,' he begged, 'it can make us rich.'

Ignacio, with his little curtain of greasy hair spread out over his skull with vain precision, actually rather amused Encarna.

'All right, but keep your paws to yourself.'

Just then, Tender Titi stood in the middle of the editorial floor and clapped his hands.

'Attention, please.' Everyone stopped writing. 'We're going

5

to have a little whip-round for champagne. The star of our magazine is going to Hollywood!'

Encarna looked daggers at him and her colleagues looked daggers at her.

'She's going to see Julio Iglesias!' Titi rolled his eyes. 'Mmmmm! How she can bear it.'

She got up, angrily. 'You're sick with envy.'

'The bald singer with the golden voice.'

Titi's ominous voice followed her as she ran down the stairs. What a prick! Better to be bald than have hair growing out of your eyebrows like certain people. But Diana Dial knew full well that, despite being on the pinnacle of fame, a receding hairline was one of the many crosses Julio Iglesias had to bear.

Down in the street she strode through the muggy Barcelona summer. Catching sight of herself in a shop window, she thought she looked a frump. She felt like stamping on her body, but instead hailed a taxi and directed him to Llongueras Unisex. *Tomorrow I'll buy some clothes more in tune with my new name and image*, she promised herself, and closed her eyes at the thought of sneakers, white tracksuits, crimson bomber jackets, suntanned skins and sparkling sets of fluoride teeth.

At thirty-two, Encarna Alférez was not pretty, and, if truth be told, she did look a bit old-fashioned, but at least you could say she had squeezed from life everything Max Factor and Helena Rubinstein had to offer. At night, every night, Encarna took off her make-up in the solitude of her flat, then spent a good hour daubing herself with assorted samples of the beauty lotions and creams that descended on the magazine. She'd been bequeathed five crows' feet at the corner of each eye by her inveterate habit of laughing even in the direst moments, but had an unshakeable faith in the miracle of cosmetics. She was still a believer, despite editing *Rumour*'s beauty pages for many years and knowing that there comes a point in the race between Woman and Time (That Monster) when only surgery and orthopaedics can help.

Encarna's life had been like a novel. At fourteen she'd begun as an apprentice in several department stores; at seventeen, a chance meeting with Viceversa's wife, whom she'd rescued at the

6

eleventh hour from buying a fake crocodile handbag, changed her destiny completely and plunged her into the fascinating world of journalism. Encarna, who in her idle moments wrote poetry, had always longed to be a journalist.

Viceversa, whose real name was Luis Brunet, recognized the girl's literary talents at once and hired her. That was fifteen years ago. Encarna had been so immersed in her work that she hadn't given a thought to a home and family. Her only love affair, if you could call it that, was with a man old enough to be her grandfather, whom she met through the magazine. Viceversa had put her in charge of the section 'Rumour Will Help You Find Your Loved One', which consisted of a couple of pages of photos of people who had disappeared without trace. Some reader always phoned to say they'd seen a person like the one in the photo somewhere or other. Encarna would then follow up the lead, find the lost person, advise the family, and skilfully capture on celluloid the happy reunion sponsored by the magazine.

The man who was to become her lover, Félix Segundo, appeared in the office one day, asked for the person who'd discovered his whereabouts, and then proceeded to slap Encarna so hard she had to go to hospital for three stitches in her jaw. It turned out that he had passed himself off as dead for years, and now had to face a nagging wife and two loving sons — one a drug addict and the other a worker priest.

With this elderly man, whom she had landed in trouble and felt responsible for, Encarna had a romance so dramatic it made her own serials pale in comparison. Félix Segundo would say: 'You're my last chance,' and though she had an awful time, she hadn't the heart to leave him — especially since he told her he would grab her by the hair and give her a bloody good thumping if she did. Luckily, he fell ill with prostate trouble and died a few months later, and Encarna consoled herself by writing stories about little old men in old folks' homes, until Viceversa called her to heel and told her to stop depressing the readers.

It was just about that time (Encarna was twenty-one) that she saw Julio Iglesias again.

She had first met him in 1971, when he came to Barcelona to

7

sing at the Poliorama for a week. The show had had to close after two days because not a soul went. Julio and Alfredo Fraile had invited the press to a private dinner before the show, and Encarna had turned up in all her finery, but Julio hadn't even noticed her. She didn't hold it against him, though. She realized that he only had eyes for his wife, Isabel Preysler, who was with him, and for the priest who had married them, who was also at the dinner and who went on to earn a good living annulling marriages in La Rota.

Depending on how you looked at it, the show's flop could have been Julio's punishment for not having noticed her at dinner. That's what Encarna thought when she was in a bitchy mood, which was rarely. She knew for a fact that Catalans didn't give a hoot for Julio Iglesias in those days and, to make matters worse, there'd been a cock-up in the publicity; the posters had got lost or something. So the night before the show opened, Alfredo Fraile, the photographer Tony Monka (who now works at *Secrets* and used to be really keen on Encarna) and the one and only Julio Iglesias himself had gone round the streets giving out free tickets so as not to be faced with the dreaded sight of empty stalls, which was what happened anyway.

Gosh, thought Encarna as she pushed open the glass doors of the Llongueras salon, *what bitter moments a star has to endure before he reaches the heights of fame*. Would Julio Iglesias have forgotten that terrible humiliation, or was it the memory of that and other failures that spurred him on to future triumphs? She sighed. Disappointed love, which the singer evoked so beautifully in his songs, must also have been a boost to his career. Just like hers.

If Encarna was a flop in the love stakes, however, it was by abstention. Since she was seventeen, since joining the magazine, almost the only love she'd come across she'd written herself in the endless romantic serials Viceversa made her conjure up, by instructions and counter-instructions. Encarna obeyed him, docilely inspired by the ambitious glint in her boss's eyes.

Eventually she had skilfully mastered every possible theme, progressing imperceptibly, with the passage of time and the relaxation of censorship, from the innuendo-packed platonic

8

relationships of her early serials to the rampant concupiscence of her later offerings. Viceversa's current instructions were rigid: 'A minimum of three screws, a long journey, and luxury, lots of luxury.'

And so, under the title 'Love and Luxury', Encarna Alférez, who had never been further than Majorca, became the Marco Polo of women's magazines. Surrounded by tourist brochures and posters of faraway places, she had made her characters screw at the door of the Taj Mahal, on the slopes of Vesuvius, up the Eiffel Tower, at the foot of the Keops pyramid, among the ruins of Knossos, in the lift at the Beverly Centre, on the roof of Milan cathedral, in one of the towers of Gaudí's Sagrada Familia and in front of the tomb of the Unknown Soldier in Paris. The passions of her fictional creatures knew no frontiers. Now whenever a man pinched her bum in the street, she felt like consulting the Michelin Guide. Her sex life was as frequent as an elephant's and as pleasurable as a hedgehog's.

That afternoon, on entering Llongueras, she felt as Eve must have felt when she stepped out into the world after discovering Adam was a twit and Paradise a fraud. Encarna smiled gratefully at the girl who offered her a trayful of sweets, while an army of pansies set to work on her skull. The sweets, she discovered, were of a special kind of paste designed for soldering jaws together and stifling cries for help. After what seemed hours, she blinked in satisfaction at the image of a short-haired, blonder and blatantly rejuvenated woman that the mirror threw back at her.

Would Julio Iglesias notice her this time?

The second time they'd seen each other, shortly after Félix Segundo had died, and Encarna was sort of in mourning, the same thing happened to her as happened to Joan Fontaine in *Letter from an Unknown Woman*, when Louis Jourdan looked at her as if trying to recall where he'd seen her face before, and she didn't dare tell him they even had a child together. That wasn't Encarna's case, of course, but she didn't have the courage to remind him of the dinner, the priest, and the flop in the Poliorama — least of all that.

This time it was at Barcelona airport; he'd just been a big hit

9

in Latin America and even Japan, where all the Japanese hummed 'A Song to Galicia' before trotting off to work for twenty hours a day. Julio got off the aircraft, radiant, and began signing autographs for the screaming girls. Encarna timidly stood aside (like Joan Fontaine) but someone from the record company took her arm and introduced her to Julio. 'This is Encarna Alférez, from the magazine *Rumour*.' And yes, she was sure, Julio blinked as he looked at her, but he didn't recognize her, and she didn't dare refresh his memory.

Later, while rehearsing in the night-club where he was to perform that night, Julio came up to her; letting go of the lapel he was stroking, he held out his right hand to Encarna, took hers and clutched it to his breast, while looking into her eyes. Overcome with emotion, Encarna lost all notion of time, and to this day, even if you paid her, she couldn't tell you which song Julio had dedicated to her on that historic occasion. But it was a sad song, was bound to be, and he wasn't even separated from his wife then, although it was rumoured that things weren't too good between them and that Isabel was well and truly fed up of being the wife of the man who sang for duchesses when what she wanted was to be a duchess so he'd sing for her.

Was it true, Encarna sometimes wondered, that Isabel never loved him, that she wasn't interested in her husband's career, that she even betrayed him (that Encarna couldn't believe), despite the fact that Julio had installed her in a posh part of Madrid, next door to his parents, so they could keep a careful eye on her? No, Encarna couldn't even believe the rumour that Preysler used to bunk off with her friend the Duchess of Cádiz, and that the two of them went out and about living it up.

All these doubts tortured Encarna, about to close a chapter of her life, as she rang the bell of Ignacio Clavé's flat.

'I've been looking at your astrological chart,' Saladino said as she came through the door. 'Things are going to go brilliantly. A famous, rich, handsome man is about to enter your life. Don't let your destructive nature get the better of you; try to keep him. A close friend of yours, whom you have sometimes unjustly scorned, will give you sound advice. Lucky days, 25th and 26th. Inauspicious days, none.'

'Don't be a moron.'

Ignacio was wearing an aubergine-coloured tunic and holding a bottle of red wine and a corkscrew.

'Hum, new hairdo.'

'And a new life. What is it you want to tell me?'

She gave a quick glance round. As usual, Clavé's flat smelt of P.S. (Permanent Spring) thanks to masses of synthetic lavender pastilles scattered over the furniture. Encarna didn't like lavender, she used an oily perfume smelling of violets, which in her moments of deepest depression helped her feel sophisticated, although on occasions she had to use it sparingly to avoid conflict with the outside world, especially taxi drivers, who would cause chaos in the street by fainting when she got the bottle out.

She wondered whether, now her image was changed, she should change her perfume too. Maybe something fresher, more punk, more ecological.

'May I smoke?' she asked, postponing the decision.

'Yes, of course,' said Ignacio amiably, since he was a naturist-type horoscopist.

They sat at the table, covered by a red-checked plastic tablecloth. Ignacio poured wine in Encarna's glass and drank water from a tumbler. Then he opened a tin of calamares for her.

'I hope these are good,' he said. 'They're left over from the magazine's Christmas offer. So is the wine. I'm not a big spender.'

He peeled himself a few almonds and began to chew them slowly, with enjoyment.

'We're going to make a pile.'

'Go on then, spit it out.'

Ignacio got up and went over to the piece of mahogany furniture that displayed his fine crystal and some disgusting bottles of marinated mushrooms and herbs. He came back with a little bottle containing a thick moss-coloured liquid. He put it on the tablecloth, took a piece of paper from his jacket pocket and waved it under Encarna's nose.

11

'This is the solution to the only serious problem Julio Iglesias has in his life. I'm referring to *baldness*.'

That was true, she thought. The only serious problem. Much worse than being left by Isabel Preysler, or the fact that his daughter was growing from girlhood to womanhood, infinitely worse than *You've never loved me, I know*, was the reality of those inert hairs, battered despite the most meticulous care, which crowned his adorable head. Every photo which reached the *Rumour* office, every new story about the state of the distressing bare patch, put Encarna in a frenzy, and gave her enemy Tender Titi new reason to vaunt the bounteous locks of his idol, El Puma. *That vulgar brute*, seethed Encarna. But it was frighteningly true. Could she imagine a totally bald Julio Iglesias? Could she stand the terrible impact of a shaven, shorn head appearing at the world's most prestigious venues? A wig was out of the question, too crude and vulgar for someone on so high a plane.

No, Julio could not be bald.

'What have you got in your hand, Ignacio?'

'Hair restorer. Or rather, *the* hair restorer.'

Encarna instinctively raised her eyes to Ignacio Clavé's pitiful bald pate, barely camouflaged by the four oily hairs punctiliously arranged on the cross.

'I didn't want to celebrate too soon,' Ignacio said, guardedly. 'Just imagine, a discovery like this has to be kept secret, or it could fall into the wrong hands. But I swear it works. Cross my heart and hope to die.'

He seemed to get a sudden inspiration. He got up and went over to the terrace. 'You remember Mabel?'

'Your dog? Of course I remember.'

'I keep her in the shed. Anyway, remember what kind of dog she is? What her hair's like?'

'Ignacio, are you bonkers?' Encarna was getting impatient. 'It's one of those smooth, rather disgusting little sausage dogs.'

'It's a short-haired, flame-coloured teckel,' corrected Clavé, with dignity. 'Take a look.'

He opened the shed door and whistled. A few moments later,

an indescribable shape jumped on Encarna's lap and began slobbering over her face.

'Bloody hell!' shrieked Encarna. 'For Christ's sake, what have you done to the poor animal?'

Mabel boasted a thick bright scarlet mane, in violent contrast to the rest of her body which still had its original hair.

'So, what d'you say?' Ignacio stood with arms akimbo. 'D'you believe me or not?'

'You gave hair restorer to your dog?' asked Encarna, incredulously.

'It's a skin treatment. Very simple, and of course, painless.'

He shut Mabel away again and came and sat next to Encarna.

'I want you to offer Julio Iglesias my new invention. This discovery is useless without a big fortune behind it, the only way to get money is for someone as famous as your idol to advertise it for us. He could even finance the development, invest money, a drop in the ocean for him but a lifeline to me. Just image! Hollywood plastered with billboards advertising *"Clavé Hair Restorer*, Julio Iglesias's choice". Who could be better than him, whose own skull suffers the torment of insidious, creeping baldness?'

'It's true,' reflected Encarna. 'He needs it more than anyone.'

'You know him well, don't you?'

'Well,' she puffed up with pride, 'I had dinner with him once, and another time he dedicated a song to me. But I don't know . . . that was a long time ago. He probably won't remember me.'

'I doubt it. You don't get that far just through talent. Being unaffected counts as well. I'm sure he's the same simple boy he was when he started. Look, when you get there, give him the bottle. If it has spectacular results, as I've not the slightest doubt it will, call me and I'll bring the formula, we'll sign the contract and you get ten per cent. Is it a deal?'

Encarna thought it a very generous offer, given that Julio's happiness was her only concern.

It was late when she left Ignacio's house with the bottle of hair restorer wrapped in a tissue in her bag. She thought about her flight to Los Angeles in less than twenty-four hours, and her heart skipped a beat. Diana Dial's big adventure was about to begin. Was she ready for it? For a brief moment she felt afraid.

If she'd seen the two shadows crouching in a nearby doorway, her fear would have turned to panic.

Enter Tender Titi

★ ★

No one on the magazine knew of Tender Titi's secret life. To his colleagues he was simply a not very well endowed forty-year-old, a repressed poofta with a rather vicious tongue, an incorruptible admirer of El Puma and old films of María Montez. Viceversa held him in some esteem because no one had ever kept the *Rumour* cuttings files so meticulously before. But this was all due to the fact that since childhood Titi had been an avid collector of film stars' photos, had had an insatiable appetite for the double bills at his local fleapit, and had been a devotee of the Sheilah Graham columns published in those days in *Fotofare*. His work at the magazine was an extension of his hobby and the realization of a dream: to get as close as possible to his childhood idols.

What nobody knew was that Titi had a lover, Moncho, a handsome but brutish bloke, younger than him, who spent the day handing out leaflets in Cera Street ('We pay the best price for gold, jewellery and pawn tickets'), and the night propping up the bar of the Panam, between bites of ancient chorizo and demijohns of Cuba Libre, fantasizing about managing artists who would make both his and his boyfriend's fortune. 'You put in the brains, I'll put in my PR talent,' he'd say to Titi. 'With your contacts it's a sure bet.'

Titi said nothing, he couldn't confess to Moncho, whose black thighs bulging under his jeans were the nearest thing to James Dean he'd ever laid hand on, that his job on *Rumour* was limited to keeping the magazine's cuttings in order.

'With all you know about El Puma and the world of show business, you should ring him up and offer to be his manager. Then we'd buy a fucking big house in some millionaire's resort, one of those with all-year-round sun and tropical fruit,' digressed Moncho.

And Titi thought, Yes, that's exactly what Dustin Hoffman's character in *Midnight Cowboy* wanted, and at the end he died, penniless, consumptive, all sorts of terrible things. How dreadful!

When Moncho learned from Titi that Encarna Alférez was being sent to the States, he got in a rage.

'But you're always telling me she's a real idiot!'

That summer night they took their usual stroll, down the Ramblas, towards than den of iniquity in Escudillers Street where you used to be able to eat for a few pesetas. The air was thick as molasses, and gusts of saltpetre and petrol rose from Colón. The Ramblas shone like the skin of an eel, and the couple's courage was fanned by the wine they'd consumed on their crawl through the local bars.

'Encarna and the bloody astrologist are plotting something,' said Titi, as he plucked the middle from his bread roll, one of the multitude of futile gestures he made to stop the implacable advance of his abdomen. 'I heard them arranging to meet at Ignacio's place tonight.'

Moncho removed the pockmarked skin of the chicken and, with greasy fingers, clutched a thigh as rosy pink as a baby's cheek.

'Where does the guy live?' he asked.

Titi told him, and he nodded as he kept an absentminded eye on the television.

'Come on, Felipe, switch channels, this is bloody awful.'

The waiter obliged, and the face of a smiling compère appeared on the screen.

'And now, just for you, the long-awaited return to our country

16

of José Luis Rodríguez, El Puma, the man who makes them swoon.'

Titi gasped. El Puma was looking straight at him as he swivelled his amazing hips.

'Hey,' said Moncho, 'I've just had an idea.'

Hours later, after Encarna Alférez had left Ignacio Clavé's flat, the two friends were still intriguing in the Clichy, a nightclub in Chinatown whose owner, Luscious Maria, had been a lover of Moncho's in the days when he still fancied women.

'My mother's son won't rest till he knows what they're up to,' said Moncho. 'And there's only one way to find out.'

'I'm not asking her. That bitch hates me.'

Moncho ignored the comment and went over to a Filipino whore who sometimes acted as hostess at the club.

'Is she going to see us or not?'

'She says to wait five minutes. She's got a visitor.'

Shortly afterwards they went through into the back room from where Luscious Maria supervised her realm. Dark and ample, she still had vestiges of the charms that had gained her her nickname, as well as a mixed assortment of jewels covering her chest and fingers. When she saw Moncho, her manner softened, though as he talked a glint of irony appeared in her eye.

'You'll never change,' she said, when Moncho finished. 'I thought boyfriends would've made you more sensible.'

Titi was about to explode, but his friend placated him with a kick under the under.

'I've waited years for an opportunity. Let me try.'

'All right,' she said. 'What d'you want me to do?'

'Every whore and queer in the world knows Luscious Maria. We just want you to find one who can tail that stupid bitch. I'll look after the rest.'

'OK. I know people over there. In Los Angeles there's more vice than you think. I can get them to help, but you have to do the graft. I can't go chasing around now.'

She smiled, put her hand on Moncho's crotch (Titi could barely refrain from belting her one) and added: 'Especially not for little birds who don't eat my seed any more.'

Diana Dial arrives in Los Angeles

★ ★

If it hadn't been for May, Diana Dial's Californian adventure would have ended before it began. May, Diana thought with gratitude, had behaved like a real friend, picking up the pieces after the Great Disappointment of her first contact with the world of Julio Iglesias.

It has to be said, however, that the journey Barcelona–New York–Los Angeles was not lacking in omens. For the whole first leg of the trip, Diana suffered violent pangs of guilt because of her frantic desire to steal the mask and slippers offered by Iberia for the comfort of its passengers. Even more embarrassing, the stewardesses didn't take their eyes off her for a minute, as if they'd guessed her intentions.

She couldn't even keep her mind on the bundle of gossip magazines she'd bought at the airport. What on earth did she care, at this crucial moment, wondering whether or not to stick the slippers in her bag, about her colleagues' investigation into a certain pop singer's latest face-lift, or the progress of a blue-blooded prince who was getting back to normal after an unfortunate car accident?

Diana Dial's heart felt the size of a walnut.

Ignacio Clavé had come to see her off at the airport with Mabel, though he'd had the good sense to wrap a scarf (from the 'A Magnificent Accessory From *Rumour*' offer) round the hairy hound's head. Ignacio gave her a big hug – a bit bigger than was proper she thought as he buried his nose in her bosom. Diana was a complete bundle of nerves, especially since she had her bag and magazines in one hand and in the other the enormous bunch of flowers Viceversa had sent to the plane. She'd been really moved (Flowers from the Boss), although she'd never been that keen on gladioli and was sure that the choice had been made deliberately by his secretary, who didn't like her much, jealous as she was of the superior culture and worldliness of Encarna Alférez, from now and for always Diana Dial.

In the air, she noticed her stomach had turned inside out, though she didn't know whether it was airsickness or pure and simple fear of the future.

The first blow came in New York; as they landed, she didn't see a single skyscraper anywhere. Of course, she rationalized immediately, they weren't going to stick them round the airports. The second setback came from the airline; her case had been sent to the Bahamas. She immediately regretted not having pinched the thingummies that had tempted her so on the plane. At least she'd have had something to cover herself with at night.

Armed with her textbook English, she dragged herself off to the Iberia lost-baggage desk, where a Latin American stewardess examined her nails as she handed out forms to the victims of luggage mix-ups, in their very resolute dozens. Particularly quarrelsome were the members of the Morrocan Olympic team (the Los Angeles Olympics were beginning the next day, almost coinciding with Julio's opening night), who complained that all their inaugural ceremony tunics were in their bags.

'Allah!' moaned a kind of Third World queen. 'I've nothing to wear for the opening.'

'Wind a sheet round you,' muttered Diana Dial, trying to keep her place. 'And d'you mind not pushing? You're jumping the queue.'

'I don't know why they let women travel,' fumed the other.

When it was finally Diana's turn, she practically fainted on top of the girl, who merely stuck a form between her teeth.

'Fill this in. If you want compensation for the contents, take the third corridor on the right, go in the second office on the left, and talk to the person there, if he hasn't gone out for a coffee or to watch his wife having her baby.'

'I give up,' whimpered Diana Dial.

Her American Airlines plane was leaving in twenty minutes. She got to the departure gate in the nick of time, galloped on to the aircraft and collapsed in her seat between the window and a huge Stetson and boots situated to the north and south of a strapping specimen of the male sex. He was the first American in her life, but Diana didn't take much notice right then, absorbed as she was by her first loss of luggage and the air hostesses' amazing hair-dos, a splendid mixture of Her Gracious Majesty's busbies and first-class letter-boxes.

She thought of a brilliant serial she could write on the theme (the luggage loss, not the hairdos), but abandoned the idea as belonging to a past she didn't wish to re-visit. Anxiety about the future shook her out of her daydream. In actual fact she was also shaken by the mighty elbowings of the yank, who was manoeuvring furiously to extract a bottle of bourbon from the depths of his hand luggage. Diana watched him ask one of the two haystack look-alikes for a glass of ice, fill it to the top, and down it in one. He repeated the operation half a dozen times, then settled his Stetson to sleep on Diana's shoulder.

'Grrrrr!' he snoared, and Diana began to understand how little countries feel when the Yanks invade them.

The stewardess's voice made her jump, and she suddenly realized she'd been asleep as well. They were about to land at Los Angeles airport. She tried to fasten her safety-belt without including the Stetson owner, who was by now lying over her knees. The truth was she paid him scant attention, since the most spectacular sight she'd ever seen in all the days, serials and soaps of her life was unfolding before her eyes.

A vast blanket of lights, a multi-coloured fairground, spread out endlessly beneath her, as if all the glow-worms in the world had come together for a beauty contest. Diana Dial held her breath. *So this is America*!

In the distance was a blaze of light which slowly took concrete

shape. Nine letters summing up a thousand dreams – HOLLY-
WOOD. A luminous word on a hillside, now almost disappear-
ing in the gathering dusk.

'Errrrggg,' burped the neighbour on her lap, still dozing. It
was a premonition, but Diana Dial took no notice.

She'd been through customs in New York and she had no
luggage to collect, so there was nothing to stop her rushing for
the exit, and diving into the first taxi, driven by an enormous-
shouldered black man whose one hand covered the whole steer-
ing-wheel.

'The Universal Amphitheatre, please,' she begged.

The driver smiled at her in the mirror. 'Argentine?'

'No, Spanish.'

'Ah, Spain. Picasso, Goya, Miró, Julio Iglesias.'

Diana Dial smiled, exultant. It was true! Even Los Angeles
taxi drivers knew her idol.

On the way from the airport to the theatre, which was in
Burbank (according to the driver), she had time to re-do her
make-up at least ten times, smoke half a pack of Winstons, and
say three Hail Marys. She finally got out on top of a hill, on a
kind of monocord stretch of lawn with nothing on it but an iron
grille, a little hut and two uniformed guards bearing only a
vague resemblance to human beings. In the distance, on the
other side of the railings, was a low spacious building, a hangar
of a newfangled futuristic design.

Diana gave her name and credentials, showed her *Rumour* press
card, and said she wanted to see Julio Iglesias.

'I've come from Spain specially,' she said importantly.

The two men did not seem impressed. One of them picked up
a phone and dialled a number. Diana couldn't understand what
he said, but there was no doubt what the face he pulled meant.

'No. Way. You can't go in. No authorization.'

She was about to try to persuade him when the man called his
mate over to help. He came out of the hut, walked towards
Diana, and clamped sausage-like fingers to her arm.

'Out of here,' he said. 'You're being a nuisance.'

Diana could do one of two things: butt the guy in the balls

(she couldn't reach any higher), or be a good girl and leave the danger zone. She opted for the second. She crossed the road and sat on the far side. The sky was bright with stars, the night silent. One of the guards, the one with the hams, was coming towards her.

'Keep off the grass,' he said menacingly.

His gaze stayed on her. He was staring at her lap, and Diana suddenly realized she still had her gladioli. Pretty revolting, but still there.

'I brought them from Spain, I swear,' she protested. 'God forbid I should pick flowers in a country that isn't mine.'

The man snarled as he walked away, no doubt disappointed. Diana leant against what appeared to be a psychedelic street lamp. She was exhausted, but she thought if she waited till the concert was over, which according to her information would be in twenty minutes' time, she might be lucky enough to see Julio come out, and could perhaps go up to him and introduce herself.

The time passed, and the audience began emerging from the building. They all seemed elated, and Diana cheered up. She knew he'd been a hit. There were groups of middle-aged women enveloped in rustling, garishly-coloured material, and couples long past forty keeping broad smiles in place between bronzed cheeks. In every female hand trembled a lovely genuine plastic rose. They were happy.

'Ah,' sighed Diana Dial. 'Just my bad luck, not being in time to witness such a triumph.'

As the people started thinning out, the journalist went up to the little hut. Not too close, just in case.

'Will Mr Iglesias be long?'

'Grrrrr,' replied the guards, in tandem.

She ran back to her observation post; the minutes dragged by. It was past midnight when the last of the Amphitheatre lights went out, and it was then she heard a voice behind her. A voice said in perfect Spanish, with a hint of an Andalucian accent: 'It's no use waiting. The stars usually go out the back way.'

The light of the street lamp picked out a dark woman of about thirty, with short black messy hair and an aggressive mouth.

'I've tried it too, but it's no use.' She had a warm smile. 'Those brutes won't let anyone in without credentials.'

She thrust out an unusually energetic hand. 'My name's Mayo. Mayo del Altiplano.'

Diana envied her, and then examined her more thoroughly. She wore a green and red flowered dress, with a skirt so tight she must have been poured into it. Her teeth shone in the dark.

'I'll give you a lift to the centre if you like. Or wherever you're staying,' she said. 'My car's all right. Not the latest model, but it works.'

She led her to an enormous Chevrolet, with a pretty battered rear end. 'It's a '64. Got class, don't you think?'

To Diana it seemed an absolute relic, a junk-heap compared to the magnificent specimens overtaking them mercilessly on the freeway.

'Have you just arrived? Where's your luggage? D'you have a place to stay?'

Diana gave her a résumé and finally said she had the addresses of a couple of hotels.

'You're crazy. There's not a single bed left in the whole of Los Angeles. The Olympics, you know. The city's chock-full of athletes,' she bragged.

The journalist said nothing. She was wondering if she'd find a nice bridge to sleep under.

'You can come to my place,' May went on. 'It's no palace, but it's OK. Look,' she interrupted herself, pointing to her left. 'That's Forest Lawn. An amazing cemetery. Buster Keaton and Stan Laurel, among others, are at eternal rest there.'

Diana shivered.

'I suppose you love cremations too. You get the best ones in this place. The stars, I mean. Very lavish. And you meet lots of important people.'

Diana thought the conversation was depressing. She also thought things were beginning to go wrong. She had imagined the mere fact of announcing she was a Spanish journalist would open all doors leading to her idol. How was she to know she'd come up against a pair of intractable minders? Julio himself

23

probably didn't know his very own compatriots were prevented from seeing him.

'It's not actually a house but a sort of hotel. Very lively, day and night. You'll like it. It's very Californian.'

They drove down into the orgy of lights. An extraordinary contraption loomed out of the darkness.

'Christ! Martians!' shrieked Diana, clutching May.

'Don't be silly. It's the spaceship from *Close Encounters of the Third Kind*. I didn't like it much. I prefer love stories, even ones with sad endings. Look, on your right, that's the house in *Psycho*. He was pretty loony, that guy. You can't imagine what you run into round here if you don't watch out.'

She was getting tired of May's chatter. Her bones were aching and her spirits flagging. To think she'd missed Julio's first show in Los Angeles. Viceversa would never forgive her.

'This is the Strip. It still has its charm.'

In a daze, Diana stared at a huge billboard. 'The Legend Lives.' It was Julio Iglesias, lolling in a dinner jacket like a Persian cat in mourning, with that smile which made Diana's hair stand on end. She saw it as a good omen, even though she'd had nothing but reasons to be depressed since she'd got to Los Angeles.

'You'll soon be tucked up in bed and tomorrow's another day,' said May, as she patted Diana's thigh affectionately.

Diana spent the rest of the journey dozing, and barely noticing the hotel whose name, The Sheikh's Delights shone out in fluorescent red between a couple of fluorescent green palm trees.

They passed a fat man sitting in Reception who let out a surprisingly feeble screech when May announced her, saying 'She's a friend of mine, she's staying awhile.' May finally stopped at a door.

'This is your room, darling. Sleep well.' And gave her a peck on the cheek.

Diana got undressed and flopped on the bed, without bothering to examine her surroundings. As she drifted into dreamland, she felt as if the floor were opening up under her.

Crazy heart

★ ★

Julio took off his sneakers and threw them on the parquet floor.
His pointer puppy Mevá, son of the beloved Hey!, jumped with
fright.

'I've got them in the palm of my hand,' cried the singer.

His press agent arrived with a Sèvres china bowl, but it took a
while to persuade Julio to put his feet in the bicarbonate and
water. As the heat began to creep up from Julio's extremities, he
smiled gratefully, his eyes closed.

'I'd give anything for a game of Space Invaders. It's so
relaxing.'

'And it's the sport of the future,' his secretary added. 'No
mental effort and you feel like God when you've won.'

'Shut up,' said Julio. 'It helps me concentrate.'

'Of course,' smarmed his secretary.

'Did you see the way she looked at me?' the singer went on.

'Oh, yes!' replied the press agent and the secretary in unison.
'Who?'

'The girl in row seventeen, looking from the stage to the
right. A little blonde, sixteen, at the most.'

'Oh, yes!'

'I want her here. Right away,' he said, peremptorily. 'I don't
have dreams, I buy them.'

The other two men looked at each other.

'Just a moment,' said the press agent.

The two lackeys withdrew behind a giant fern. The secretary took out a coin and tossed it.

'Heads!' he roared, triumphantly, 'you find her.'

'Damn,' growled the press agent, 'how the hell am I going to find her at this time of night? I don't even know who she is, what she's called, what she looks like, how much she charges, if she has a boyfriend or not, if she really was at the concert.'

'That's what you're paid for.'

'True.'

From the lounge came a buzzing noise.

'Zzzzzzz.'

Julio was asleep, his mouth open.

'Saved,' said the press agent.

'You South Americans have all the luck.'

To the buzzing was added a sublime intermittent snoring in C minor. The singer was totally zonked.

A *disturbing dream*

★ ★

Julio is at the top of a hill and Diana Dial is trying to reach him.
Julio is sitting on a folding chair with his name on the back
wearing the rollers that fluff out his hair before each perform-
ance. Diana, moved by the sight, hugs the bottle of hair restorer
to her breast. For nights she has been trying to fight her way
through the dense undergrowth of the wood, but incomprehensi-
bly she makes no progress. Thousands of hands clutch at her
clothes, claw at her flesh, preventing her going any further.
Hundreds of smooth shiny faces come between her and her idol.

Queen Elizabeth sets about her with her handbag. Diana
fights her off, but the sovereign then takes off her hat, a vast
yellow model with stuffed doves on top, and attacks her with this
powerful weapon, shaking her mercilessly. As she collapses
under the weight of this pasting, she hears the voice of Viceversa
from above. 'The Queen of England, wearing an exquisite model
specially designed for her, presided over Diana Dial's inaugura-
tion ceremony in Los Angeles, accompanied by her family and
the cream of the international jet set.'

When she comes to, with the bottle buried deep in her bra,
Diana Dial starts back up the hill again, following the halo of
light emanating from Julio's rollers. Suddenly, a pack of Vatican
cardinals surround her and silence her by threatening her with
huge incense holders. One of the cardinals, the tallest, points to

27

the small group which has just formed in a clearing and which at first Diana mistakenly takes to be the Holy Family: it turns out to be Lech Walesa and his wife, well and truly pregnant, who kneel before Pope Wojtyla while he blesses the bulging belly. 'We should put him on the cover,' she hears Viceversa say. 'This Pope sells more than Julio Iglesias.' Diana wants to shout but her throat won't cooperate.

The cardinals have disappeared and, in their place, Stephanie and Caroline of Monaco try to strangle her with their respective bikinis. Out of the undergrowth comes Carmen Martínez-Bordiú de Rossi brandishing a seventeenth-century wall clock and is just about to smash it over Diana's head when the voice of Jean-Marie, the famous antique dealer, stops her. 'Careful! It's a piece of incalculable value.'

Defeated, on her knees amid pine needles which tear her skin, Diana sobs with bitterness. When did Fabiola give up the idea of motherhood, when did her sister-in-law Paola decide to stop gambolling around fashionable beaches in pursuit of a gigolo, when did the last Kennedy die, when did Cristina Onassis eat Maxim's out of caviare? Viceversa's questions thunder against her brain but Diana's mind is a blank, she only knows that Julio Iglesias is up there, crooning a gentle love song, and that she has to reach him before it's too late, before Vaitiare or Sidne Rome or one of his usual companions close in with their steam-heated curling-tongs and ruin the little hair he has left.

But just then a pop star and a bullfighter, whom she can't identify because they're in plain clothes, hurl themselves at her, grab her ankles and bring her down on the grass again. Luckily the bottle seems safe and doesn't spill a drop, but unluckily her body is beginning to feel the effects of such an uneven battle, and again she hears Viceversa's voice, increasingly like the voice of God, asking for eight pages to accompany the photos of Gunilla Von Bismarck dancing in Marbella.

The charming image of Julio in rollers begins to vanish. Diana shouts, 'Wait!' though she doesn't know if he can hear her. It is then that an ominous shadow, an unmistakably Filipino shadow, settles herself firmly on the slope, impossible to go up, impossible to pass the sphinx holding an enigmatic tape recorder and a copy of *Hello!* (*Rumour*'s competitor) like a sharp weapon. Isabel Preysler barely moves a facial muscle as she threatens Diana.

'Don't kid yourself, titch. The only woman in Julio Iglesias's life is me. And I predicted he'd go bald ages ago.'

The others have come back too, the Pope, the cardinals nod piously, the Walesas kneel in prayer before Preysler, Queen Elizabeth and Lady Di and Stephanie and Caroline and Jacqueline and Cristina, poor little rich girl, form a ring round the former Mrs Iglesias, and bicker over who has the honour of crowning Empress the woman who has been on the most magazine covers this year.

I must do something, mutters Diana Dial to herself. And suddenly she finds a matchbox in her hand, furtively takes out a match, strikes it, holds it to His Holiness's skirt and, in a matter of seconds, the papier-mâché figures begin to burn, and they burn and burn, and keep on buring till they're all reduced to ashes.

Mayo del Altiplano's Working Day

★ ★

Mayo del Altiplano had learned to suck cocks from her step-father, in a slum in Granada, the city where she was born twenty-nine years ago. Like Diana Dial, the name Mayo used wasn't her real one, but she'd changed it so long ago she no longer remembered what hers was. In any case, who cared? When she was still a kid, she sucked her way to Barcelona, and the city was putrid enough then for her to feel quite at home practising her favourite pastime and earning money into the bargain. Not much, but enough to get by, and that was a lot for someone who'd grown up among foul-smelling shacks.

Later she crossed the ocean to Mexico, but didn't stay there long. Her dream was to go to Hollywood and become a star.

That was ten years ago. Now she was in Hollywood, and all she'd acquired was an old Chevy, a credit card with a $500 limit, a job in Fatty Flop's sauna, and her name translated to May of the Mountains.

Her work consisted of entertaining clients, singing at night in the sordid club in the basement and rendering some service or other to regular customers who were too inadequate, ugly, or boring to pick up someone for themselves in the sauna.

Flop said May was a gem, and May didn't at all mind contributing to the Californian dream by licking the goolies of lonely, depressed guys who came to the Sheikh's Delights for the

30

illusion of feeling desired. It was her Mother Teresa side, May knew that.

In the club, however, she could be something else. An artist. Make up and dress up like famous stars, impersonate them or, for the trickier ones, mime to a recording. She'd been good at impersonation ever since her days in *Barcelona by Night*, warming up the Catalan bourgeoisie and intellectuals who came to the club looking for a bit of verbal sadism and moderate perversion.

She'd made good friends during that period. Luscious Maria was the best. Luscious Maria was one of those whores who'd never enjoyed sex, a true genius in the art of controlling the other person's pleasure for her own ends. She took a fancy to May, although she never tried it on. She just gave her good advice and passed on the occasional lucrative trick, almost always performed in the posh parts of town, discreetly, with no names asked. Maria also knew how to get dazzling clothes at half price and old jokes that, brought up to date, did wonders for May's part of the show.

Everything would have gone swimmingly if some old boy hadn't decided to cop it as she was rendering a service and Luscious Maria hadn't thought it best to put a few thousand miles between them. May had to go, first to Mexico and then to Los Angeles.

Not that she lamented her fate now. She'd discovered two things: that Hollywood was the place where more illusions died than anywhere, and that surviving your own illusions was a feat few could manage. May had done it.

She'd also discovered she liked that particular pantheon. To feel comfy in it, all you had to do was get used to the idea that you were a worm.

Luscious Maria's phone call brought a spark of adventure into her life again.

'I need you,' Maria said. 'Don't let me down.'

And so the previous night she had tracked down the Spanish girl outside the Amphitheatre. It wasn't difficult, because Maria had given her a good description and, besides, Diana's scared-rabbit look gave her away. The problem was what the hell to do with her for the next few days. Luscious Maria had promised to call with new instructions.

'God,' moaned the guy she was sucking in Room 103. 'God, I'm coming.'

She rinsed her mouth with mineral water and spat it out over the sauna coals. *Pffff*. She went out, leaving the guy panting.

Flop was in the reception, as usual, tidying a pile of towels. He suffered from insomnia and, according to him, it was a blessing from God. He was a fundamentalist, so anything which helped his business was a gift from heaven.

'Your friend's still sleeping.'

'Leave her alone. She must be tired out.'

Fatso shrugged the blubber that served as his shoulders. 'Fine by me . . . . Ernie's waiting in 107.'

'Complete service?' asked May.

'Apparently.'

Ernie was one who liked first-class sex, but he paid well. She picked up a towel and disappeared down the hall.

The Sheikh's Delights

★ ★

Diana Dial woke up with the sensation that the MGM lion was sitting on her head. The sun, streaming in through the window, burnt her eyelids. She drew the curtains but the brightness still pierced everything.

Sitting on the edge of the bed, she remembered:

One, I'm in America.

Two, I haven't seen Julio Iglesias.

Three, Viceversa will be livid.

Her heart went into her mouth. *I am in America. In America.* She rushed to the window, pulled back the curtain and stuck her nose against the glass. She was on the ground floor, and the street outside the window was one she'd seen in at least a dozen films. A supermarket. A gas station. A black woman sitting on a bench poking around in a paper bag. A Seven-Up ad. Cars.

She dressed hurriedly in the only clothes she had, sniffing them with disgust. *I'll have to buy something till they send my case,* she thought. She slung her bag over her shoulder and left the room.

The hallway was long and narrow, between two rows of doors with numbers on. It was diabolically hot, and the dark-red carpet oozed grease. The hallway lead into a smallish room, which she vaguely remembered; it was furnished with a bluey-green three-piece suite, shelves full of towels, a reception desk,

33

and the fattest man she'd ever seen puffing away as if he was trying to race round himself.

'Hi,' said fatty.

'Where's . . . ?' she tried to remember.

'May? Room 107. But she's working.'

Diana suddenly had a feverish desire to get back to work too. She had to find Julio Iglesias, then she'd ring Viceversa and try to soothe him with some tale or other. The main thing was to track down her idol. Perhaps her new friend could help her.

She opened the door of 107 without knocking and said, 'Mayo, can you . . . ? What on earth are you doing?'

'Giving a client an arse job,' replied May.

'Ahhhhhhhhhh!'

Diana shut the door and leaned against the wall. She was just pulling herself together when May came out, zipping up her jeans.

'You . . . '

May shrugged her shoulders. 'No one's perfect.'

Bastard, thought Diana. Couldn't even say anything original; that belonged to the end of *Some Like It Hot*.

'Had breakfast?' asked May, picking a hair out of her mouth. 'I'll just get my bag, we'll go across the road for a coffee.'

'It's disgusting,' said Diana afterwards, pensively.

'Yes, it's really bad here,' May nodded to the coffee urns in front of her.

'No, I mean what you did. Tricking me like that.'

'Listen,' said May impatiently. 'You were lost and I took you in. Yes or no?'

'Yes,' admitted Diana.

'Well, don't complain, for fuck's sake. As far as I know, there wasn't anything between us. Or are you into girls?'

Diana felt like crying. She was alone in Los Angeles and her only help was a bloody great Andalucian whore with the dick of a truck driver.

'Why does everything have to go wrong?' she wailed.

'Come on, don't be a prude. This is Hollywood, people see things differently here. Here, dry your eyes, I've got a surprise for you.'

34

She followed her reluctantly to the door. 'Where are we going?'

'To a top-notch cremation. Fred Stark died yesterday in the Cedars of Lebanon. A cirrhosis the size of a cathedral. The funeral's today. Everyone will be there.'

'I've a pile of things to do,' protested Diana. 'I have to find Julio and . . . '

It was useless. When May of the Mountains saw the chance of a cremation on the horizon, nothing in the world would sway her off course.

'Don't worry. We're bound to meet someone there who can help.'

She piled her in the Chevy and set off at top speed. They went down Santa Monica and turned down Vine Street towards Hollywood Boulevard.

'That's Paramount Studios, but I'll show you another time. We'll just about make it.'

She stopped the car a few metres from a small crowd clustered around an imposing black marble façade.

'See? They're on the dot. Those are the fans, but we're not staying in the street.'

With an air of authority, she led Diana through the crowd. May had put on black glasses and adopted the solemn bearing of someone who has just suffered a great loss. They crossed a huge colonnade and went into a vaulted room full of people dressed as if they were at a wedding. May guided her along a pink marble wall.

'We can see from here,' she said when they reached the far end of the room. 'Look at the faces. I bet you've never seen so much fame in one place.'

It was true. She could see Rock Hudson, looking very ill, Dyan Cannon, Shirley MacLaine, Linda Evans, Joan Collins, Pamela Sue Allen . . . She was overwhelmed, so many personalities.

'It's fantastic,' she murmured. 'And her?'

She meant a tall woman dressed in black, her face hidden by a veil.

'It's Sarah Stark, the widow. They were at daggers drawn, but any widow worth her salt has to attend her husband's funeral. She's well provided for and is free to chase toy-boys now.'

The coffin was resting on top of podium covered with crimson velvet.

'Let's get closer,' May said.

Fred Stark lay on a plain white bed of lilies. They had buried him in the uniform of an officer of the Seventh Cavalry, a role he'd brought to the screen so often, and his crossed hands lay on a gleaming sword. His lips and cheeks were bright with rouge and his lashes thick with mascara. A shock of very black hair fell over his forehead. Diana could have sworn it moved.

A preacher began his speech. Diana caught only a few odd phrases: 'Heroes die on their feet,' 'We will always remember his talent,' 'Quiet dignity in the face of illness,' and things like that. When the priest finished, a vault opened automatically in the back wall and the coffin began to slip inside.

'Now they're going to burn him,' explained May, emotionally. 'It's cleanest and surest, besides, you can put the ashes anywhere.'

Just then, a superhuman cry broke the respectful silence. Before anyone could stop her, the widow threw herself on the coffin and tried with all her might to stop it.

'No! No!' she bellowed.

The priest made a slight gesture, and the coffin stopped.

'No! Not the sword!' screamed the widow, frantically undoing the belt holding the weapon to her husband's body. 'The sword belonged to General Custer and is worth its weight in gold.'

In the struggle, Fred Stark's toupée had slipped and now hid part of his face, which had also started to run in rivulets of rose make-up.

'Poor Enrico,' said May.

'Who's Enrico?'

'A friend of mine who works here, doing up the corpses. That witch has ruined his work of art.'

36

Diana felt queasy. 'I've got to go out,' she said. 'I'm going to faint.'

'OK,' replied May. 'But you won't want me to miss *this*.'

And she pointed to the crowd which, with sudden enthusiasm, clustered around the widow, chanting in solidarity: 'The sword! The sword.'

She fled the temple as best she could, feeling more and more queasy. She waited for May on the pavement, minimally protected from the implacable Californian sun by the shadow of a palm tree which waved above her.

Forty minutes later, May came up smiling beatifically.

'It was magnificent. Half of them have fainted, including the widow. Oof, there's nothing like a good cremation to make you feel better. To make you feel alive in this bloody city.' She lit a cigarette. 'Now I'm going to repay your patience by showing you round Los Angeles. You've just trodden sacred soil, you know. Lots of stars have had their funerals here, from Thomas Ince to Bela Lugosi. And poor Peg. She wasn't a star, of course, but she had a fascinating death. Want to hear it?'

She didn't try to resist. She knew it was useless.

'In those days, Hollywood, well, the sign had four more letters. Hollywoodland. And poor Peg climbed on the last D and threw herself off.'

'Why?'

'What d'you mean, why? Because she'd failed, in the city of her dreams. So she spat her death at Hollywood from the very top,' she said, with obvious enjoyment. 'Don't you think it's marvellous?'

'It gives me goose-flesh.'

In actual fact, what was making her hair stand on end was the thought of Viceversa's tantrum if she didn't get in touch with Julio soon.

'I know how you can find him,' May said suddenly, she sometimes had the knack of reading thoughts. 'My friend Enrico, the one who makes-up corpses, just told me. Julio's living in Bel Air, but it's absolutely impossible to get in, the

37

security is scary. The best thing to do is speak to his press agent, who's staying at the Sheraton with the rest of the crew.'

After all, May wasn't really a bad girl. Or a bad bloke. Or whatever.

The book

★ ★

After she'd spoken to the press agent, Diana Dial, exultant now, asked for a line to Spain, which Flop provided despite roaring that this wasn't a hotel, nor was he a telephonist.

'Where the devil have you got to?' said Viceversa amiably.

'Calm down, boss. Everything's going perfectly. I missed last night's concert because the plane was late, but I've got my seat for tonight.'

'Terrible. I mean, brilliant,' he congratulated her, in his own inimitable way. 'Now listen. I don't want you to do the articles I asked for.'

'Fine. How many pages?' asked Diana. To interpret Viceversa's orders, all you had to do was understand the opposite of what he said.

But this time he was serious: 'I want you to concentrate on collecting material for a book. Find out all you can, make notes, and come back when you think you've got enough material.'

Heavens! A book. *Her*?

'It'll be the book of the year,' insisted Viceversa. 'We'll call it *The Intimate Truth About Julio Iglesias*, or something of the sort. It will be your definitive consecration.'

He *wants to consecrate me. My boss.*

'Any news?' she asked, in honeyed tones. *Now he'll say he misses me, that I'm an invaluable part of the magazine, that he's going to leave his wife for me.*

'Everything's going great.'

She said nothing, disappointed. Or did Viceversa mean exactly the opposite?

'Just one thing,' said Viceversa.

'What?' *Now, now*, wished Diana, closing her eyes, her heart piercing her blouse.

'Ignacio Clavé has disappeared. He should've brought me this week's horoscope yesterday and he didn't turn up. I sent a boy for him and he found the flat in a mess, furniture all over the place and not a trace of Clavé. I had to print last year's horoscope for the same dates.'

'Have you told the police?' Diana asked, anxiously. 'What's happened to Mabel?'

'I didn't know he was married.'

'Mabel's his dog.'

'Dog? It must be a lion,' said Viceversa. 'Apparently his flat was covered in hairs.'

'Oh, poor Ignacio! Poor Mabel!'

Viceversa hung up before she burst into tears, so he didn't have to console her no doubt. Men!

The anxiety in the pit of her stomach over the fate of Ignacio soon gave way to jelly at the thought of the book Viceversa had commissioned. It wasn't that she wasn't pleased. A biography of Julio Iglesias! Not in her Snow Whitest of moments could she have imagined anything like it. Finally giving up serials and fantasy, getting to grips with the most exciting of all experiences: Life. And not any old life, but someone who's forehead had been touched by the magic wand of Fate. She hurriedly wrote that last sentence down. Ah, Literature, she mused.

What tormented Diana was not the book itself but her lack of confidence in herself. Would *she*, a former salesgirl, be capable of describing in all its splendour the triumphant existence of the most extraordinary singer of all times? Could *she* trace with enough drama the milestones in Julio Iglesias's road to glory, from the time he was thrown out of his school choir, to July 18,

1968, when he won the Benidorm Song Festival with the incomparable theme entitled 'Life is Still the Same'?

Diana burned with desire to tell someone. She went off to find May, hoping she wasn't busy with one of her tricks.

'Fantastic!' gushed the transvestite, who was painting her toenails in the solitude of her room. 'Take the shaver off the chair, make yourself comfy, and tell me everything.'

Diana only obeyed the third command, and pacing nervously about in the space left by piles of May's clothes on the floor, she told her friend the latest news.

'Can you imagine? The chance of a lifetime! Much better than those articles, which, after all, appear in any old magazine. A book is something unique, personal. The present I've always wanted to give Julio.'

'You have to talk to him,' advised May. 'How can you write it if you don't see him.'

'I'm going to his concert tonight. Sorry you can't come, but I've only got one invitation.'

'Doesn't matter, I have to do my act anyway. If I were you I'd buy myself something decent, something stunning.'

'Yes, of course. I can't go like this.'

May gave her the address of some downtown department stores where the end of month sales had begun, and Diana rushed round them like a bat out of hell. Two hours later, she left the shop with a gold lamé sheath two sizes too small for her, shoes to match with twelve centimetres of stiletto, and a champagne-coloured synthetic mink stole. She also plundered the make-up department. *What the hell*, she thought.

She gave herself time to stroll round the centre, watch the antics in Pershing Square, and marvel at the baroque lobby of the Biltmore Hotel, packed with Olympic competitors in their national costumes. At a news-stand, she bought the *Hollywood Reporter*; practically the whole thing was devoted to Julio Iglesias. On every page were notices welcoming him to Los Angeles. Restaurant owners, hairdressers, personal friends, singers, composers, agents . . . all wishing him luck.

And she, thought Diana Dial, was going to share in that luck.

41

Because, deep down, she and Julio were the same: two fighters, two people who'd come from rags to riches, though in the singer's case, his success had been astronomical. She trembled with pleasure.

Back at the Sheikh's Delights, May could barely spare her a glance. She was immersed in the opening ceremony of the Olympics on television. Next to her, Flop was stuffing fistfuls of popcorn into his mouth from a carton the size of a skip.

'The athletes are so cute,' cried May. 'Just look at those thighs.'

Diana went off to her bedroom, ready to do battle with the lamé. She felt like Miss America.

Dreams of seduction

★ ★

This time she walked up to the guards like a queen.

'Mr Iglesias is expecting me,' she said, waving the invitation gracefully.

One of the heavies, the very same one who had pawed her the night before, lead her to the stage door. She crossed a sort of cement patio to a little building stuck on the side of the main structure. A bloke in civvies, with a Studio security system badge in his lapel, examined her pass and showed her into a small foyer. Diana was glad she'd dressed so elegantly.

Among those standing waiting, chatting to each other, were the cream of the television soaps Encarna Alférez devoured in her faroff Spain. Telly Savalas, Linda Evans, Jane Wyman, Charlene Tilton . . . If Viceversa could see me now, she thought. A tall, corpulent man, holding a beer, came up to her.

'I'm Julio's secretary.'

'I'm Diana Dial from *Rumour*.' She showed him her card.

'It says Encarna Alférez.'

'A printing error. Don't you see the photo?' she replied, drily.

He introduced her to the press agent.

'Yes, we spoke on the phone.'

He was a young man, with a bird-like head and piercing eyes.

'Go to the bar, and get yourself a drink. I'll take you in when the show starts.'

She settled herself in a corner, by the bar. The little room seethed with blonde women bejewelled up to their eyebrows and men with damask jackets and shoulders as broad as wardrobes. All had a drink in their hand and an ear to ear smile.

'Who are you?' A slim girl, with a mane of chestnut hair, looked at her with curiosity.

She introduced herself.

'I'm Silvia,' said the girl. 'Alfredo's secretary. Want a drink?'

'No, thank you. I'm hoping to see Julio.'

'You will, don't worry. He's impossible not to see.'

'Hey, that's Joan Collins, isn't it? We were at the same funeral this morning.'

'Someone you know died?'

'A relative.'

It wasn't the moment for explanations.

So this is Hollywood, she told herself. It wasn't the faceless corpses May had talked so much about, nor the ageing out-of-work stars going to the supermarket on their bikes in rollers; no, Hollywood was here, in the few square metres of the foyer to the idol's dressing-room. Perfectly made-up faces, arranged harmoniously over cascading jewels, unwrinkled sun-bronzed skins, insultingly white teeth, firm taut breasts emerging from the softest fabrics Diana had ever seen, sculptured male heads of silver or jet held arrogantly high, the obligatory Cartier on every wrist and the swish of complicity from Calvin Klein underwear.

The press agent led her into the Amphitheatre. 'You can't grumble. It's one of the best seats.'

In the darkness, she felt the presence of the crowd, shouting, sweating, stamping impatiently. Someone sat beside her. She turned to find Dr Iglesias. He examined her with scrutiny.

'You're a journalist, aren't you? You like my son? Of course you do. You'll never have seen anything like this.'

The stage was an explosion of light and music, but it was empty, empty of him, of Julio, and Diana crossed her fingers and thought of Viceversa, the magazine, all the serials she'd ever written, Ignacio and Mabel, poor things, Tender Titi and even Félix Segundo, God rest his soul, and the hard time he'd given

44

her. The memories shrank to a distant point among the mass of romantic images projected on to the back of the stage: flower-filled meadows, snow-capped mountains, ripe ears of corn waving in the breeze.

Julio came on. Diana was ready to drink her fill of him like someone taking communion. With serenity. He advanced delicately to the front of the stage and was drowned in the female roar that rose from the stalls.

'Let's see,' he said.

His voice.

'How many Spanish speakers are here tonight?'

His bearing.

'How many Italians?'

His gaze.

'How many French?'

His smile.

'How many Americans?'

His black suit.

'You all speak English, so you won't mind me talking to you in English.'

His international style.

Dr Iglesias was gripping her arm. He was hurting her, but Diana Dial didn't notice. She only had eyes for Julio, up there on the stage, laying his hands on his heart, then stretching them out towards the audience, as if in prayer.

His songs.

She lost all notion of time, she delivered herself up.

'So much feeling,' said Dr Iglesias, clutching her knee with both hands.

Julio was serenading love. Diana felt the love at that moment. Loss, desertion, disillusion. Starting over again. Gone with the wind. In short, 'The Fundamental Things of Life'.

She didn't see the Mexican teenagers screaming at their idol to notice them, nor the Japanese girls in kimonos carrying little American flags, nor the buxom matrons crushing their programmes to their blubbery bosoms, nor the middle-aged gentlemen discreetly patting their stomachs to confirm sadly that they weren't as flat as Julio's.

'Why do women love me?' Julio was musing, philosophically, at that moment. Then louder to the audience.

'Because you're handsoooooome!' shouted the Mexican teenagers.

'No, no, no, no. I'm not handsome. I'm too thin and I can't make love like I used to.'

'Yeeeeeees! Yeeeeees!' they all roared. 'Make love to me!'

Ten minutes of that. At last, the idol gave in and carried on singing, stopping in mid-sentence to direct words like 'I love you' and 'You're terrific' at the audience.

What good English he speaks, thought Diana; *even I understand him*.

'I feel very proud to sing for you, for the great American people,' Julio was saying, 'the greatest country in the world, and I'm happy you have taken me to your hearts as if I were one of you. You know,' he crossed his legs on the stool, 'I used not to sing very well in English, because I didn't feel it. I used to say gueerl. Now I've learned to say guirl. Guiiirl, guiiirl, guiiirl. I feel it comes from here.' And he pointed to his heart.

The house came down.

On her way backstage again after the show, Diana's right side was black and blue from Dr Iglesias's effusiveness, but her spirits were soaring. Were there words to describe the historic concert she had just witnessed? 'Tell them what you've seen, so in Spain they'll know once and for all who my son is,' the friendly doctor had recommended, accompanied by one last pinch. Oh, yes. But, will I be up to it? She should have taken notes, she told herself, cursing the lack of foresight which brought her to the concert without a bloody notebook. She went to the toilet and wrote some odd words on loo paper: apotheosis, vulnerability, masterly stage presence, polyglot. Just enough to reproduce an memorable occasion in the book.

Backstage were the same people as before, and a few more added. They looked just like the others, fresh from the mould. She saw Alfredo Fraile, the manager, smiling beatifically, the press agent, the rest of the entourage. The secretary went in and

46

out of Julio's dressing room, laughing nervously. The guests devoured canapés and champagne.

'Lovely.'

'Marvellous.'

'Exciting.'

'Sexy.'

'Latin.'

'Lover.'

At last silence fell, and Julio Iglesias came out of his dressing room, dressed all in white, his freshly wet hair combed back, his arms open, an apparently natural peel of laughter.

'Ha, ha, ha, ha.'

Everyone clapped. Everyone surged towards him. His minders had to introduce a bit of order. Kisses, congratulations, manes of blonde hair waving.

'These people are very, very important in show business,' someone told Diana.

'I know.'

Someone pushed her, and her eyes met Julio's nose. It was Diana Dial's great moment.

'*Atchoo*!' sneezed the singer.

'Bless you!' said Diana.

The mêlée carried her away from him. She elbowed her way forward, desperately trying to recuperate lost ground, to get back to Julio and bathe in his shining eyes, his honeyed voice. It was hopeless. Between Diana and her idol floated a tide of de luxe admirers also trying to get near him, and doing it with more success than her.

'Are you coming to the party?' Alfredo Fraile was beside her.

'What party?'

'A charity gala. I'll tell them to take you in a car.'

'Are all . . . all these famous people going?'

'And lots more,' smiled Alfredo.

A party in the Mecca of Cinema! And she, Diana Dial, dressed from head to toe in gold lamé.

Political interlude

★ ★

Nancy Reagan helped the President off with the bullet-proof vest protecting his precious life, folded it, and put it away with a sigh in the chest of drawers in the bedroom of their Rancho del Cielo in Santa Barbara.

Ronnie, liberated, flopped in his favourite armchair, under the stuffed head of Tyrone Power, his main rival in the days when the great statesman had been a film actor. On the President's lap lay the torch with which the Olympic flame had been lit at the opening ceremony of the Games that afternoon.

'It was magnificent.'

'Oh, yes,' said Nancy. 'Very patriotic.'

'Now those dirty Soviets will know what kind of a country they're dealing with.'

'A bit of music?' suggested Nancy, going over to the stereo.

'Put on "Up with People", "Let's all go to the promised land", or something like that. I feel folksy today.'

'I prefer something of Huuuuulio's.'

'You know I like him a lot, darling, and whenever he comes by the White House, I love seeing him. Besides, he brings in Latin votes, and heaven knows we need them. But I still say that Andalucian's bad luck.'

'He's not Andalucian, Ronnie. He's Basque.'

'Well, same thing.'

'He's not bad luck, darling. That's you being silly.'

'Silly, eh? He sang for Sadat on September 7th, and on October 10th, he was assassinated. And poor Grace, one of ours even, had a heart attack while she was listening to a cassette of his in the car.'

'That hasn't been proved.'

'And don't forget Torrijos, he was a friend of his, and Somoza, he'd sung for him too.'

Nancy shrugged her shoulders.

'You're going gaga. Look at Pinochet, strong as an ox.'

'We'll see. Anyway, I don't want to expose myself more than I have to, just in case.'

With anorexic tenacity, Nancy picked up the album *Julio* and took the record out of its sleeve.

'You may be the strongman in politics, but at home I wear the trousers.'

Ronnie got up, took his bullet-proof vest out of the chest of drawers and put it back on. Then he took off his hearing-aid and put it on the bedside table.

'If the Democrats could see me now,' he grumbled.

Tinsel town glitz

★ ★

The salons of the Sheraton Première sparkle with glittering chandeliers and magnificent gilt mirrors, and with the added brilliance of perfect teeth, taut cheeks, pinched eyelids, flattened double chins, stomachs smoothed by the miracle of suction, backs massaged at $100 an hour, groins hardened by aerobics, and multicoloured glasses that barely camouflage the satisfaction and pride of belonging to the Hollywood colony.

When Diana Dial enters the hotel, tripping along in the massive stride of one of Julio's minions, she knows she is an intruder, that people the world over would give years of their life to attend a happening like this.

'Come on, let's eat,' says her guide, and drags her towards a huge buffet piled high with delicacies of the kind Diana had only ever seen in the food sections of magazines, and even there nothing as fabulous as what her eyes now beheld: avocados big as pumpkins, crayfish big as crocodiles, and oysters you could stage 'Holiday on Ice' in. *It's natural*, thinks Diana, *that everything should be bigger in America, bigger and better for people whom seem lovelier, and happier to be alive.*

Her guide has two plates and is filling them when an unmistakable crescendo of murmurs, like the clamour of a tribe of cannibals getting ready to dine, announces that something is about to happen, and the guide hands the two plates to Diana, tells her to fend for herself, and shoots off towards the entrance, throwing his huge carcass against the crowd, very much in the style of a handball player, which is in fact what he was before working for Julio, though Diana thinks Julio would be better off with a rugby champ to defend him from the hounding of his innumerable fans.

Clutching her plates, Diana Dial watches a compact group advance towards the centre of the salon, and manages, with difficulty, to distinguish Julio's unrivalled smile, his tanned skin – infinitely more tanned than anyone else's, and this at the Sheraton on a night when no one could admit to not owning a mansion with a swimming pool.

And – Diana can't believe it – at Julio's side, also smiling, is Brooke Shields, the most pampered of all juvenile stars, who only a few days earlier appeared in the papers as Michael Jackson's new girlfriend. Ah, sighed Diana, the singer with the golden voice has managed to supplant the teenagers' idol in the affections of America's latest sweetheart.

So Julio enters the Sheraton Première arm in arm with Brooke Shields and her mother, who looks at the two of them enraptured, as does the rest of the assembled gathering, on their feet, their private conversations interrupted. Hollywood takes him to its heart, thinks Diana Dial, and truly, seeing him so handsome, so well groomed, so elegant in his white linen suit, his whole success embodied in the perfection of his smile, Diana understands that Julio is part of that world where even the food is a different size, like success or happiness.

'He reminds me of Philippe Junot, but more passionate,' exclaims a lady, fluttering her eyelashes.

'And more refined,' adds her friend. 'I have it on good authority that he's an aristocrat from a very old family.'

Diana, who by now has abandoned the plates, walks between the tables in a daze, and sees how the clan members crowd round Julio and look at each other quizzically, they are clearly concerned about his welfare. Julio, Brooke, and the presumed mother-in-law sit at the same table, in the centre of the salon. Diana goes as near as she can. Jesus, how beautiful they are.

51

Brooke murmurs something in the idol's ear and he gives the genuine Julio Iglesias guffaw which the photographers rush over to immortalize.

Outside, in the lobby, stoical hostesses are handing out cardboard cubes with Julio's face engraved on each side. Seeing that the boxes are given in exchange for a ticket, Diana plucks up courage and asks in a peremptory tone for her box, her treasure. What can it contain that makes such elegant ladies go away delighted with their booty? The hostess asks for her ticket, there is a bit of argy-bargy, finally they believe her ('I'm Julio's guest, would I be here otherwise?'), they hand it over and Diana rushes to the door labelled Rest Room. Thank God for the lamé, which makes a nobody into a lady.

Alone, in the toilets, sitting on the seat, Diana rips open the box, her hands tremble as, one by one, she pulls out the fetishes: an LP and a cassette with songs by Julio Iglesias, two lipsticks, a pot of eye shadow, some Estée Lauder perfume, a serviette-ring heavy as a bad conscience and, biggest treasure of all, a photo album of Julio, colour pictures of him singing with his eyes closed and an expression of infinite suffering, with his eyes open and a smile of unbridled hope, with his naked torso (His Torso) leaning against the wall of one of the rooms of his sumptuous mansion in Miami, on board his extraordinary yacht *Chabeli II* (what a gesture, naming his boat after his beloved daughter), pensive at the piano (is he contemplating the terrible solitude of an idol in a crowd?), in a Rudolph Valentino turban, greeting Prince Rainier of Monaco and his wife Grace, God bless her soul, chatting with President Sadat, Allah bless him, walking alone down the aisle of a theatre, getting dressed, getting undressed, in front of the pyramids, beside the sphinx, with his dog, with his kids, another one with his dog, another one with his kids, and even with a little black boy who looks at him with admiration.

As Diana Dial comes out of the ladies, loaded down with her priceless trophies, she doesn't even notice Angie Dickinson who brushes past her with a hip seemingly made of tin, or Fernando Allende, the revelation of *Flamingo Road*, who is coming out of the gents doing up his flies.

The party is almost over, everyone seems to have forgotten about her, and Diana Dial has to call a taxi back to the Sheikh's Delights.

Setbacks

✦ ✦

'HE IS A MAN WHOSE PASSION INFLAMES EVERYTHING HE DOES. HE MADE HIMSELF WALK WHEN HE WAS TOLD HE WOULD NEVER WALK AGAIN. ONLY PASSION CAN PROVIDE THE DRIVE TO SPEND 1,800 HOURS IN A STUDIO PRODUCING AN ALBUM, OR RECORD IN FRENCH, ITALIAN, GERMAN, JAPANESE, PORTU-GUESE AND, FINALLY, IN ENGLISH, OR GO ON TOUR FOREVER, OR FACE FAILURE IN THE UNKNOWN WATERS OF AMERICA INSTEAD OF STAYING ON SAFE TERRITORY, THAT IS, IN THE REST OF THE WORLD.'

Diana translated with difficulty, following the review in the *Hollywood Reporter* with her forefinger, and with the same finger of the other hand, wiping away her drooling.

'AND THERE HE IS, ON STAGE. HE CARESSES THE WORDS WITH CONTROLLED PASSION AND DRIVES THE AUDIENCE INTO A FRENZY. THEY SAY THAT IN VAR-IOUS MIDDLE EASTERN WARS BOTH SIDES CAN BE HEARD PLAYING JULIO'S CASSETTES. IT'S POSSIBLE . . . THEY ALSO SAY THAT A SONG OF HIS IS HEARD SOMEWHERE IN THE WORLD EVERY 30 SECONDS, AND THAT HIS MUSIC KNOWS NO FRONTIERS. THE NUN ARRANGING FLOWERS ON THE ALTAR SINGS THEM, SO

54

DOES THE FRENCH FARMER WHO GETS UP AT FOUR IN
THE MORNING. A ENORMOUS RANGE OF PEOPLE SING
THEM, FROM YOUNGSTERS RACING MOTORBIKES
DOWN THE NARROW STREETS OF MILAN TO HOUSE-
WIVES IN CUBA, AND FROM NOW ON, TEXAS TEE-
NAGERS IN JEANS, AND MILLIONS OF LOVERS.'

Diana devoured the Yankee literature devoted to her idol, her
face still smeared with traces of her night cream.

'THERE IS EVEN A SPANISH GIRL WHO MEASURES
DISTANCES IN TERMS OF JULIO'S SONGS: "FOUR AND A
HALF JULIO IGLESIAS CASSETTES FROM CANGAS TO
MADRID." BUT THE PASSION CONSUMING JULIO
RECENTLY IS TO BE ACCEPTED INTO THE HEARTS AND
HOMES OF AMERICA.'

I'll never be able to write anything so perfect, she thought,
dejectedly. *Viceversa will sack me, and what's worse, I'll be an object
of ridicule for Julio and his important friends.* Lying on her bed, she
listened to America waking up. Horns near by, in the distance
sirens. Sirens near by, horns in the distance. She'd left the
curtains open, and to her surprise, she realized that nobody
looked in anyway. In fact, there were hardly any passersby, and
when cars stopped at the lights, they showed her only the
indifferent profiles of their occupants. 'Los Angeles is a proces-
sion of cars, pilgrims getting where they're going to along a
network of freeways, without realizing they are forming a
strange cathedral, the biggest, most mobile and most spectacular
church in the world,' May had told her the day before, in one of
her moments of applied philosophy.

May. She could never think of May as a woman again, having
seen what she had between her legs. Nor could she think of her as
a man. So how could she explain the friendship she was beginning to feel, the affection her eyes and even her tits provoked,
but which changed to excitement when she imagined her below
the belt? She wondered whether it was a bisexual feeling. Or
don't feelings have a sex? That's a good question, worthy of a

55

spot in the agony column (or sexologist) of *Rumour*.

A knock at the door and May's hoarse, vibrant voice: 'Are you awake?'

'Come in.'

May burst into the room wearing a silk robe, bobby pins in her hair, and tennis shoes.

'Surprise, surprise. Iberia have sent your case. It's in my room. Since you got back so late last night . . .'

She rushed over to get her luggage. Back in her room, with May beside her, she began to unpack.

'What lovely clothes,' said May. 'Will you lend me some?'

'Pick whatever you want,' offered Diana, taking out dresses, make-up bags, shoes, her dowry bought specially for the New World.

With no more ado, Mayo put on a set of salmon-coloured satin undies and began pirouetting round the room.

'You'd look better without the tennis shoes,' commented Diana. Good Friend.

Suddenly, she stopped. 'Shit!'

'What is it?'

'Something's missing.'

'Anything important?'

'Very important.' The time had come to confide in May of the Mountains. She told her.

'Hair restorer? For Julio Iglesias? She burst out laughing. 'That really *is* a good idea.'

Diana sat on the bed, hunched over. 'Think Iberia will give it back?'

'If they've done something as impossible as getting your bag back, the rest doesn't seem so absurd.'

'In that case . . .'

'What?'

'Something else is missing too.'

'Let me guess. A miraculous cream to fix Julio's skin; he certainly needs it.'

'No, it's something of mine. Something very private.'

'Photos? Letters? A diary? A lock of your lover's hair?'

'A vibrator.'

'A comforter?' May's eyes popped out of her head. 'I'll be damned. You sly old thing.'

'I was very fond of it,' confessed Diana. 'It was from the *"Rumour* Solves Your Needs" offer, which in the end we didn't dare publish.'

'I'll phone Iberia. Just tell me what it was like. Though quite honestly I don't suppose many get lost.'

'Pink, with two speeds, and when it's on a little bulb on the end lights up.'

'Better just ask for the hair restorer. The other thing, anyone can do you one in this city.'

Diana sighed. That was Another Problem she'd have to face some day.

Inventor in a jam

★ ★

A smell of stale vegetables and beaten eggs came creeping in through the window giving out onto the stair well, presaging the advent of the evening meal. Ignacio Clavé's rumbling stomach, empty for a day and a half, firmly supported this premonition. His wrists and ankles hurt from the ropes that disgusting individual had tied him up with. Lying on the floor, in a foetal position, Ignacio tried to remember if his horoscope had foreseen anything particularly nasty for yesterday. It was hopeless. His mind was completely blank. And a profound desire to retch welled nauseously up from his stomach and prevented him calling for help.

He thought of Mabel, of the pitiful way the dog had done a runner. True she had tried to attack the assailant at one stage, but when she saw that the situation was desperate, she slunk off without a shred of dignity. Man's best friend indeed!

On the morning of the dreaded attack, Ignacio was making breakfast of cereal and distilled water when the doorbell rang.

'Who is it?' he asked before opening; he was naturally prudent and these days you never knew who you might find on the other side of the threshold.

'I've a message from Encarna Alférez,' said a male voice. 'I need to talk to you.'

He opened the door, and zap! A six-foot brute with bully written all over him.

He knew he'd made a mistake even before the guy held the knife to his throat. Mabel came trotting in from the kitchen, but Ignacio knew only too well what a vicious beast *she* was. He didn't keep her shut in to stop her attacking strangers, but so she wouldn't run off with them.

Mabel ran to the brute's feet and gave them a friendly sniff, snorting with pleasure. Meanwhile, Ignacio was being taken at knife-point to a corner between the sideboard and the fridge.

'From Albacete?' he asked, trying to gain time.

'What?'

'The knife, it's beautiful.'

'Albacete, my arse. Now, let's hear it; what shady fiddle are you and Encarna up to?'

'We're just good friends,' he whined, feeling the steel tip probe his jugular. 'I'm doing her astrological chart.'

'You motherfucker!' To add insult to blasphemy, it was accompanied by a kick in the crotch.

Ignacio doubled over and the brute had the decency to lower the knife a bit, just enough to follow the line of his neck without puncturing it. With his free hand, he began pounding the body, until the astrologer sank to the floor in a tattered heap.

'Mercy,' he begged.

The intruder looked down at him mockingly from his intolerable height. Mabel, still licking his feet, broke off every now and again to give Ignacio a wet kiss or two now she had his face at her level.

'Bloody animal,' said the villain, kicking out at the dog.

About time he did something decent, thought Clavé, looking at Mabel with primeval hatred. The pooch didn't seem to like the intruder's gesture, because she growled, showing her teeth. Another kick. Another warning from the dog. *Perhaps he'll forget about me*, prayed Ignacio. Mabel flung herself at the villain's ankle and he waved the knife at her. Unused to knives, Mabel backed away. She looked at Ignacio, shook her exuberant mane and galloped off towards the door, which was still open.

59

They're all the same, decided Ignacio, and finally felt too weak to face the foot that was being lifted menacingly again.

'I'll tell you everything.'

'That's better.'

He blabbed all about the hair restorer and his plans to persuade Julio Iglesias to use and promote it.

'What a great idea!' said the brute admiringly.

'Isn't it? I've invested a lifetime in this invention. Ever since my hair started falling out. One Columbus Day, to be exact.'

Ignacio wasn't as stupid as the other guy might think, so he told him Encarna had flown to Los Angeles with the hair restorer and the formula. He was careful not to tell him that, for security's sake, he always kept the document with him, in his underpants, in a little bag he'd made himself.

'All right,' said the intruder. 'Don't worry, I'm not going to hurt you. But you're coming with me. I'm taking you somewhere you can't foil our plans.'

He led him from the flat, bound and blindfolded. The lady next door, who was sweeping the landing, greeted him cheerfully:

'Ah, Don Ignacio, practising again?'

Ignacio cursed the day he'd tried to impress her by doing the Houdini trick of escaping from a trunk bound by chains.

His assailant put him in the back of a van parked in front of the building. From then on, it was all darkness and banging. When they reached what Clavé supposed was their destination, his body ached all over from the potholes.

They went down several steps (him bumping down), from which Clavé deduced he was going to be locked in a cellar. He heard the clink of keys, the creak of a padlock, was given a push in the back, and a door slammed shut behind him.

'Can you take the blindfold off?'

The other man obeyed in silence. Ignacio looked round. Four bare walls, except for last year's calendar of a naked girl, and patches of damp. A small window at ceiling level. No chair or stool Clavé could stand on to look outside.

'Lie down.'

60

Now he's going to rape and murder me, Ignacio imagined, horror-struck. *Or he'll murder me first, then rape me*, he imagined, even more horror-struck. But all the guy did was tie his ankles together. Then he gagged him.

'You'll stay here nice and quiet for a while.' He checked the ropes were tight enough and then gave him an almost friendly thump on the back, just hard enough to leave a bruise.

'You're a clairvoyant, you could have predicted it,' he muttered before he locked the door.

Ignacio had been tied up like this for a day and a half now, and though he'd struggled enough to loosen the ropes slightly, he was still a prisoner like in the first volume of *The Count of Monte Cristo*. To make things worse, he'd drooled so much that the gag had tightened, and stuck to the roof of his palate, making him want to retch.

His pangs of hunger were sharpened by the symphony of sounds descending from the kitchens. He knew he was in the cellar of a block of flats in a slum area. But which one? By refining his pituitary gland, he came to the conclusion it could only be Chinatown or Barceloneta, but the profusion of children's voices told him it was the latter. Besides, every now and then, in gusts, he got a whiff of the sea.

How long would he have to stay there? Would someone save him? Would he die of starvation like some wretched macrobiotic? Just as he was about to make a fortune, thanks to his brilliant plan.

He dozed off thinking of a great big plate of bean shoots and sesame.

'*Grrrrr*.'

He was shaken out of his daze. The noise came again.

'*Grrrrr*.'

He looked round. Nothing.

'*Grrrr, rrrrr*.'

Mabel! Ignacio saw her little face against the window pane, looking down at him, and his first thought was that she parted her hair on the side since she'd been gone. But then he stopped thinking, because someone was forcing the door. Seconds later,

61

Mabel, Viceversa and his chauffeur were making a triumphant entrance into his dungeon.

'God Almighty, what a dump!' exclaimed the boss. 'I bet you're pleased?'

'How did you get here?' asked Ignacio, once he'd got his gag and rope off.

'The dog. She came to the office and caused such a rumpus they tied her to a table leg. Then I . . . ahem, said the best thing was to let her go, and follow.'

Master and beast hugged each other tight.

'Hey, let's go to the office – we've got some desperate Cancers writing letters of complaint.'

Clavé put his hands together in prayer. 'I feel dreadful, I'm a bag of nerves, boss. I need a month's holiday.'

And since Viceversa had a heart of gold, he agreed. Everything was set for Ignacio Clavé to begin the second volume of *The Count of Monte Cristo*. His revenge.

Afternoon in the Sheraton

★ ★

'I'm a hooligan. That's why Julio hired me as his press agent.'

Diana Dial gathered her skirt and crossed her legs, nodding in agreement, although she'd no idea what he meant. May had dropped her in front of the Universal Sheraton, after insisting on another tour of Los Angeles. As they drove down freeways more like runways, and streets more like freeways, she started on her favourite subject: the history of Hollywood seen through its murders, suicides, deaths from boredom and deaths from grief.

'This city is one big cemetery,' she had said. 'Look at the houses in the suburbs. They're mausoleums with thirty metres of lawn. There's not a single bird, because there are no insects left; they'd spray your soul with insecticide before they'd let you ruin their garden. A garden no one goes in. Their children don't make messes, and their dogs don't do poos.'

Diana was barely listening, absorbed in her own problems, of which the loss of the hair restorer wasn't even the most important. To hell with Ignacio (what happened to him, by the way?) and his dotty schemes. The serious problem was the book. Would Julio Iglesias agree to see her? Would she, Diana Dial, get the chance to talk to him face to face? Everything seemed easy in Spain, but the journalist realized things were very different here. Her idol's superstar status put a barrier between him and his only remotely similar fellow creatures.

63

She said goodbye to May, kissed her on a cheek freshly shaved and smelling of Chaleurs de Femme, and reached the Sheraton reception desk after a heroic trek across the lobby, desperately trying not to sink into the ten centimetres of soft pile, or panic because the chandelier worthy of the last scene of *Phantom of the Opera* might fall on her. And now she was by the pool, next to the press agent and the others, trying to understand what he was saying to her.

Thank goodness she looked smart, in a wonderfully creased unbleached linen suit, which gave her Confidence In Herself.

'So you want to interview Julio. And write a book about him. Bloody hell, that all?'

Diana lowered her eyes, humbly.

'That's pretty difficult. In fact, I'm here to make sure no one interviews him, see? If I do my job properly you interview me instead of him.'

Alvaro, the photographer, and Silvia, the girl Diana had met the previous night, gave each other knowing looks. With them was a guy Diana hadn't seen before, who was introduced as Ray, the group's manager. He just did sums in a notebook, with a slight smile.

'As I was saying,' the press agent went on, 'when journalists want to write an article about Julio, they ask me. Julio's not available. Julio lives in his own world. He's an artist, understand? I can tell you what he has for breakfast, what kind of girls he likes, why he always wears black socks. You know, all the things the public wants to know.'

'It's true,' agreed Diana, visibly moved. 'Julio can't waste his time. But if you say I'm Spanish, perhaps . . .'

'Darling,' said the agent. 'Darling, we've got the Spanish press in the bag. Julio has a direct line to the owner of *Hola!*, Jaime Peñafiel is a close friend of his, and the rest will sell their grannies for any bit of news and a couple of his photos I send them.'

He gestured to Alvaro. 'The only press we're interested in at the moment,' he went on, 'is the British, German, Brazilian, Japanese and, of course, the US.'

'So, there's no hope?'

'We can try. Though I don't promise anything. It'll take time. Staying long?'

'As long as it takes,' she perked up. 'My boss has given me *carte blanche*. You can tell Julio we met in Spain in '71, and . . .'

'I know. I know everything. Whenever journalists want to speak to Julio, I get all the low-down on them. A telex with all their particulars: who they are, professional status, what they've written about Julio before, and what we can expect in the future.'

'How amazing,' gushed Diana, 'how efficient!'

'Yes, the best reports come from Japan, from CBS there. So,' he smiled, 'you don't have to tell me who you are.'

A shiver of anxiety ran down Diana's spine, but the brief moment of alarm passed in the admiration such perfection inspired. How fascinating, she thought, the world of the artist. How thrilling it would be to see his way of life, the secrets of his private self, take shape in her immortal book.

Alvaro yawned visibly. 'This is fucking boring,' he said. 'Let's change the scenery, at least. Let's go to the bar.'

They dragged themselves off inside. Diana followed them, fascinated. She was getting to know Their World.

Two very young blonde girls appeared, twittering. The press agent signalled to them.

'Come here, girls. The bad thing about hotels,' he turned to Diana, 'is they're very tiring. Moving your arse from one place to another all day. In the end all hotels look the same. So do the women. Take these, for instance. Don't worry, they don't understand Spanish. They don't understand anything, in fact, but they fuck pretty well. Isn't that right, baby?' he added. 'Tell me, d'you love me for myself, or because I'm Julio Iglesias's press agent?'

The girls just smiled.

'A couple of tickets for the show and they're happy as Larry.'

'He inherits them,' said Alvaro. 'Then doesn't even pass them on.'

Diana felt a bit out of the conversation. In fact, these intimate details seemed to her A Bit Sordid. Show-business stuff, she thought, benevolently.

'Help! Help! Nikitaka!' a female voice shouted just then.

The whole group stood up.

'Shit! The Jap!' they exclaimed in unison, as a diminutive oriental girl dressed in silk came tumbling into the bar.

She flung herself into their arms, sobbing. 'My bag's been stolen! My bag, with my ticket for Julio's concert.'

'We can sort that out, my little one.' The press agent took a piece of paper out of his shirt pocket and gave it to her. The girl threw herself at his feet in gratitude, and then left the way she'd come in, except backwards, bowing.

'She's the president of the Tokyo fan club. A saint. She works twelve hours a day teaching English, and everything she earns she spends on trips to see Julio sing.'

Alvaro interrupted him: 'Hey, I'm going to the launderette.' He turned to Diana. 'This toff pays our hotel room, but not the extras. And laundry in the Sheraton costs a fucking arm and a leg.'

Diana thought him very vulgar. She ignored him and said, 'I'm going to put all this in my book.'

'About the launderette.'

'No, the Japanese girl.'

'OK, OK. We'll see what we can do, sweetie.'

The meeting

May had told her she'd take her to the beach on Sunday, and she did. 'They'll have to manage without me in the sauna today. I'm free until tonight's show.'

They threw their swimsuits on the back seat of the Chevy and went down La Cienaga on to Venice Boulevard. They stopped at a liquor store to buy cigarettes and magazines and May bought a sticker of Barbie as a nurse for Diana to stick on her bag. While May drove (with her right hand, her left leaning lazily on the window), Diana admired the graceful palm trees, so still in the sultry heat.

'Los Angeles has lots of nice things. Good weather all year round, and knowing no one gives a damn about you,' philosophized May. 'Don't say it's not fantastic, the feeling there's no idiot after you.'

The boulevard ended abruptly near the sea. They found a space in the municipal parking, next to the used caravans sale.

'Now you're going to see a really weird place,' announced May. 'This area of Los Angeles is called Venice, because the guy who built it at the beginning of the century wanted to imitate Venice, Italy. Look, most of the canals have been filled in, and the few that are left are dry or full of stagnant water. His dream of Venice sunk.'

They walked under the colonnades, which reproduced with

childish candor those of San Mark's Square. On the walls were huge paintings of dollar bills, or a nude skater imitating Botticelli's Venus, or simply the scenery opposite, like a set of worn mirrors. All showed signs of age.

'The trendies of each generation have come to Venice, from the beatniks to the punks, and each generation has dumped a part of its hopes and shit here. During the day it's fun, everyone has a ball. There are sunbathers, beach bums, vendors, and break-dance freaks. At night the real inhabitants come out. It'd break your heart to see them. It even makes my flesh creep, and I can cope with anything.'

They crossed Ocean Front Walk, with its kilometres of stalls, and got changed in a cement hut which stank of urine. Then they walked to the water's edge and spread their towel among the mass of bodies.

They lay on their backs. Diana stared at May's bikini bottom. 'What have you done with . . . ?'

'An old trick. I stick it behind. I may put it back in its proper place before I leave. You don't know what to do for a pick-up these days.'

The water was shallow, Diana had to walk out quite a way before she could swim. It was tepid and oily, but, well, it was the first ocean she'd ever seen, and she ducked under like a baby at a baptism. Under the water the silence engulfed her like a womb and, when her head came up, the abrupt sound of a language she didn't always understand hit her. Children shouting, defiant voices of athletic boys leaping like dolphins. It was unreal.

She went back to May. Later they ate hamburgers and drank beers wrapped in paper bags. 'To protect the poor minors, they've made California laws fucking absurd,' May informed her. Diana felt drowsy and dropped off. When she woke up, with her friend shaking her, she thought she was returning from a long trip. She'd dreamed about Viceversa.

'Hey, you're red as a lobster. Better cover up.'

She put on a T-shirt with a picture of Donald Duck. 'I'm going for a walk,' she said.

She crossed the wide fringe of tanned bodies, sheets (*Califor-*

nians aren't too keen on beach towels, she thought), surfboards
resting like prehistoric squid, bottles of suntan lotion, empty
Coca-Cola cans, and coloured umbrellas. She joined the beachfront just where the break-dance experts were showing off for a
crowd of fans who, judging by the shouting, seemed more like
the bookies she'd seen in films.

That part of the beachfront, packed with stalls and peddlars,
stretched from the fake St Mark's Place as far as the eye could see
towards Santa Monica. Diana let her eyes lead her on, all agog,
like a little girl lost in a bazaar. People selling perfume, orientals
versed in acupuncture, tarot-card readers, sexologists with on-
the-spot diagnosis, tattoo artists, and snake charmers whose
snakes were sceptically asleep in their baskets. Africans peace-
fully hawking fake ivory carvings alongside kids selling T-shirts
printed with portraits of the illustrious dead (*May was right*, she
thought, *here the dead are more important than the living*), trashy
novelties, stickers, photos, smuggled electronic goods, melons
and water-melons. It was like any other market in the world, but
with the space and races multiplied a million-fold. It was Diana's
first contact with the American spirit of free enterprise, so it was
impossible for her to distinguish between buying and selling and
what appeared to be one big party.

She just watched in fascination, believing in the profound
truth of what she was seeing, just as she believed in the genuine
flavour of the huge pale blue-coloured ice-cream she was licking
with gusto now, and in the beauty of the bodies walking by her,
bodies of ebony or milk chocolate or amber or gardenia, jet-black
hair plaited in impossibly tiny pigtails, or diaphanous manes of
burnished gold waving in the wind, cheeks of blush pink or
polished black marble, all with that huge wide-eyed look of
astonishment at being young and free in Venice at the weekend.

The man who was watching her, leaning against the wall of a
pizza parlour, had the inevitable brown paper bag in his left
hand, the neck of a bottle poking out, and he looked as if he
didn't believe in anything at all. Dirty, matted grey hair and
beard, a faded Hawaiian shirt hanging out of some pitiful ragged
jeans. Diana averted her eyes and mingled with a group of

69

youngsters waiting for a fortune teller with a silver ring in her nose to read palms.

She went on for hours, for kilometres, until she realized her calves were aching and it was time to turn back. The sun was by now a huge orange floating on the horizon to her right, and the beach was almost deserted. The air smelt of hamburger fat, coconut oil and rotting raw fish. It was the pungent tang of the ocean mixed with the excrescence the visitors had dumped on its shore.

Back at the spot she had left that morning, May was nowhere to be seen. She walked left and right looking for him. The enormous carpet of sunbathers had disappeared as if by magic, only the sand was left, strewn with rubbish. She sat down, disillusioned, but it was cold on the beach now, so she went back to the promenade and tried to figure out the way to the car-park. The second-hand caravans were still there, but no sign of the Chevy.

She imagined May must've picked up a handsome beach-bum and would be letting his instincts loose in the back seat of a car. She decided to wait for him in The Walk, the only café with a terrace she'd seen on the way, just in front of the Pavilion. *He has to come by here*, she told herself.

She managed to get a seat at a little corner table, the only one free in the noisy crowd munching salads covered in pink sauce. She ordered a coffee and expected May to materialize at any moment with a triumphant smile on his face. But he didn't. And very slowly Diana began getting worried. If May had gone off with just anybody, how the hell was *she* going to get back to the sauna? She didn't even know the exact number of Santa Monica Boulevard the Sheikh's Delights was at, although it probably wasn't difficult to find. But anyway, how was she going to get there from Venice? *Don't be silly*, she thought. *How can A Journalist get lost?*

It was now totally dark and the café clientele was starting to leave. A cold wind blew in from the sea, and all she had on was a T-shirt and bikini bottom. Most of the stalls were packing up, so she took a decision: to buy something warm before she caught the stupidest and most inconvenient pneumonia of her life.

The last stalls looked as if they were having closing-down sales. She chose a pair of army-surplus trousers and a jacket. The clothes were too big for her, but she felt comfortable and warm in them. All around her, Venice was emptying quickly. The human wave that had taken over the coast was ebbing back inland.

She hesitated. She didn't know what to do. Leave, or give May one last chance? He couldn't have just abandoned her like this, and taken her clothes.

She started walking north. The road was littered with paper and empty drink cartons. Two black guys, leaning on a lamp-post, watched her dopily. She walked past groups of people sitting on the ground, people who in no way resembled those she'd seen purring in the sun earlier in the day. These were not glorious specimens but human scraps, emerging from the darkness in clothes that didn't seem to belong to them but floated reluctantly around them like unruly shadows.

Diana felt afraid, but at the same time fascinated; she wanted to stand there watching, as if these fragments of another story were about to come together right there to reveal something to her.

As she walked further into the darkness, the pathetic wail of a clarinet came out of nowhere to improvise a duet with the boom of the waves. Bewitched by the two sounds, she had that same sensation of unreality she'd felt on the beach. But now it was different. Now she recognized what was around her. She'd seen men and women like these in Barcelona, in Chinatown. She'd seen them slump to the ground on a corner, tired of walking or living, or both, and drag themselves to the door of one of the few bars that let them in, down as they were on the very lowest rung.

A man pushed a rickety pram full of rattling bottles towards her. As he passed, he clutched her arm, muttering incoherent words. Diana shook herself free, and the man walked on humming.

She stopped, listening to last notes of the clarinet.

'You alone?'

She felt a whiff of alcohol waft across her face and, even before

71

the faint light of the street lamp confirmed it, she knew the man speaking to her was the one who'd stared at her in the market, the one whose eyes seemed not to believe anything.

Diana Dial wanted to scream. She was Alone In America. Quick as a flash, she tried to imagine how a heroine in one of her notorious series would react in A Situation Like This. 'Excuse me, but I don't think we've been introduced.' How silly that all seemed now. The best thing would be to turn and run, but the guy seemed to have lost his arrogance and besides, under his eyes, those sceptical eyes, he had two delicate mottled patches of tiny blue veins that reminded her of Félix Segundo and his pathetic attempts to behave badly when he tried to stop her leaving him.

'A girl like you shouldn't be walking alone in a place like this.'

She still said nothing. She tried, meanwhile, to put on an intrepid-explorer air, but realized she couldn't fool him. There are Unexpected Events which even a naïve young end-of-season sales addict can recognize, and one of them is the supreme moment in which a Real Man appears in your life. So Diana Dial took a deep breath and said nothing, absolutely nothing.

'See that old guy?' he went on. 'He looks inoffensive enough, but in his pocket is a flick knife that can cut a boar's throat. He'd stick it in your heart for a couple of dollars and those earrings.'

'They're fake,' explained Diana, hurriedly.

'Even so, it's more than he's ever had. Come on.'

He took her hand. 'Let's get away from the beach.'

They walked back to the Square. The arches, which during the day had framed the swaying hips of stately Blacks carrying huge radios, were now piled high with rubbish. He led her through the narrow unpaved streets and then across a precarious little bridge without a handrail, which straddled a stream.

'Careful,' he said. 'It's rotten with damp, and if you slip and fall in, you'll catch all sorts of nasty things.'

They came to an open space where the only two houses, shoulder to shoulder, seemed trying to shore up their respective ruins.

'That's where I live,' announced the man. 'And next door,

impossible though it may seem, Allen Ginsberg used to teach. That was a long time ago, mind you.'

Diana refrained from asking who that friend of his was. There were lots of things she didn't know but, as Viceversa wisely advised her, a timely silence can save you from ridicule in Any Situation.

The man pushed her gently into one of the buildings, the most decrepit looking. Diana held her breath but thought it a bit late to practise the second golden rule her mother had taught her when she started walking to school alone; don't talk to strangers. The first golden rule (although chronologically Diana received it later, when her period started) referred to the inadvisability of conceding favours for any reason whatsoever ('They love you, and leave you,' her mother used to say), and Diana sensed she wouldn't be following that one tonight either.

Because, what the hell, despite the bad breath and the filthy clothes, this stranger did have something special, something that declared her body under siege; a mixture of cheek and pathos, an irresistible cocktail of three parts wretchedness and one part pride that Diana had only seen on the screen. And his lips were the icing on the cake, the softest and sexiest she'd been near, including Viceversa's, which in their dynamic executive variant weren't bad either.

They climbed some stairs with creaking steps, he opened the door which also creaked and, then, went into a bedroom which more than creaking was like Pompeii in mid eruption.

She had to use all her strength of character not to obey another of her mother's golden rules: roll her sleeves up and give this pigsty the Feminine Touch all bachelor pads need.

She couldn't have done it anyway, because the stranger flung himself at her and began pawing her newly acquired battledress panting expressively.

'I fancied you the moment I saw you, my little lamb,' he roared, in perfect Spanish.

'What a coincidence,' she moaned, returning with relief to the language of Corin Tellado.

'You fancy me too?' he asked, taking his incisors out of her neck for a moment.

'No, I mean what a coincidence you speak such good Spanish.'

'I should, I'm from Bilbao.'

It's strange how, when the Great Opportunity comes, you're hardly ever aware of it, mused Diana Dial afterwards, as she smoked a cigarette her new friend had just rolled. In theory, after all that shouting and ecstasy, *it* should have worked. Of course, there was what she preferred to call Her Other Problem, but while it was perfectly logical that Félix Segundo and the few other pathetic men who'd occasionally shared her bed couldn't solve it, there was absolutely no reason why a Great Big Basque like the one who'd just given her such a thorough going over shouldn't have got to the Root of the Problem.

Why did she still miss her exquisite rose vibrator, sadly lost by an Iberia blunder?

As usually happens in these cases, Diana got maternal, stroked the man's curly hair and said: 'Don't worry, it's not your fault.'

He looked at her, perplexed. 'I had a great time.'

'Me too,' she hurried to reassure him. She wasn't altogether pretending. It had been, by a long way, the best roll in the hay she could remember. Nevertheless, something was still missing. And deep down she felt sad.

'What's wrong?' he asked, getting up. 'You women all get droopy after a good fuck.'

His naked body was nervous and skinny, although a bit pot-bellied. Diana figured he was about forty – not a very good forty, of course. He found a transistor and a bottle of bourbon and came back to bed.

'D'you like music? Want a drink?'

Diana said, 'Yes and no,' and he made a face.

'Don't drink? Pity. A bit of liquor helps to keep the chords tuned.' He lolled back on the mattress and stared at the ceiling.

'I knew you were a compatriot right away, soon as I saw you.'

She smiled at him sweetly.

'You know, "Spanish women and horses, small heads and fat arses." ' He buried his face in Diana's neck. 'I've been dreaming of an arse like this for years.'

74

It wasn't exactly what she'd wanted to hear, but she was in no position to be choosy. Besides, she felt utterly content beside him, so much so that she had an incredible urge to tell him her life story.

However, before she could, he began to tell her his.

'You're probably wondering what I'm doing here, where I'm from, how I got into this shit.'

'Diana wasn't wondering anything at all (except why on earth *It* hadn't worked), but she nodded, understandingly.

'You're looking at a guy who used to have a new car every year, and a flat on Park Avenue. The top people in the pop world passed through my office.'

He turned up the transistor, from which some gang of imbeciles was mouthing things like 'Love me now, baby, there's no tomorrow.'

'The only thing I've ever been good at is selling other people's music. I would've liked to write my own,' he smiled, 'but I've no creative talent. I was pretty shrewd at the other, though. I still am, but it's too late now.'

He stroked her breasts. Diana regretted not having been more assiduous in her use of the Firm Breast Ampoules which *Rumour* recommended to its readers. He went on.

'I began in Bilbao, over twenty years ago, promoting local groups, but soon moved to Madrid. There I joined a record company and soon got to the top of my field. The Americans noticed me. It was like a dream. CBS hired me. They first sent me to Paris to let off steam, then to Miami in charge of the company's Hispanic artists, and finally, the big break, to New York. It was when Clive Davis had people like Simon and Garfunkel, Blood, Sweat and Tears, etcetera, under contract. Great times. That sentimental music, all that melodic crap, seemed dead and gone for ever.'

A voice shrieked out of the transistor: 'Gimme a bitta love, baby, stop thinking of the future.'

'I like a good tune,' said Diana Dial, staunchly.

His fingers stopped over her left tit. 'Don't tell me, baby. Frank Sinatra and that rubbish?'

'I prefer Julio Iglesias.' She adopted an authoritative air. 'I consider his contribution to the field of romantic music has been decisive because . . . '

She stopped. The guy had got up and was putting on his trousers.

'What's wrong? I'm going to write a book about Julio. It's more interesting than you imagine, I swear.'

'Get dressed,' he said. 'Get dressed, dammit.'

He wasn't joking, so Diana stuffed herself into her battledress as best she could, took the bag he handed her, followed him down the stairs, back along the road they'd come by, and when they reached the Square, he stopped.

'End of story. Where d'you live?'

Diana told him.

'There's a bus-stop across the road. It leaves you in Santa Monica Boulevard. You can't miss it.'

Diana was dumb-struck. The guy looked her over from top to toe.

'What an idiot I am!' he muttered. 'The best arse I've come across in ages and it has to belong to a Julio Iglesias groupie. I suppose you're president of one of his fan clubs?'

'No,' stammered Diana, 'I'm just a journalist.'

'Good job,' said the guy, and turned and disappeared into the night.

The bus took thirty-five minutes to the corner of Santa Monica and La Cienaga. From there, Diana had only to walk a hundred metres through pimps, whores, and drug dealers, before laying her troubles to rest in the Sheikh's Delights, the best sauna in Southeast Hollywood.

High hopes

★ ★

'And I don't even know his name,' bemoaned Diana when she'd finished her tale.

By then it was three in the morning and May of the Mountains was taking off her Scarlett-O'Hara-visiting-Rhett-Butler-in-prison costume, which she'd worn for her act at the sauna club.

'You should've seen me,' May had rattled out at Diana when she charged into her room in her furious but pitiful state. 'I've always said that my supreme acting moment is when I *am* Scarlett fighting for the future of her beloved Tara. Or when, chewing on a turnip, I swear before God I'll never be hungry again.'

'It was a radish. What kind of girlfriend are you anyway?'

'Boyfriend,' corrected May stupidly, because he usually referred to himself as both sexes indiscriminately.

'How could you abandon me to my fate in such a spooky place?' She slumped on to the bed.

'Don't be so tragic. Journalists should know how to get around. Besides, you should've seen the gorgeous beach-bum I picked up. The spitting image of Jayne Mansfield's last husband, God rest her soul.'

Diana Dial burst into tears. May ran over to her, arranged his ample crinoline next to her, and held her in his powerful arms.

'Tell me what happened.'

So Diana told him, not skipping a single detail.

'Well,' said May with his usual good sense, 'I don't know if you're crying because you didn't come, or because you're not going to see him again.'

'I'm used to not coming,' sobbed Diana.

'Then it's crystal clear. You fancy this guy. Don't worry. He knows where you live. If he's keen, he'll turn up. A Basque in Venice. Honestly, this country is full of surprises.'

'What am I going to do?' wailed Diana, helplessly.

'Go and get your beauty sleep. Tomorrow you're lunching with Julio Iglesias. His press agent called tonight, and naturally I said you'd go.'

'Oh, that's wonderful.' Diana's tears evaporated.

'And more good news; Iberia found your famous bottle of hair restorer and sent it over. It's on the chest of drawers in your room.'

'Oh, that's fantastic.' Happiness shone in Diana Dial's face.

'Now help me get this damn corset off, the whalebones are puncturing my ribs. If I'd been born in the nineteenth century, I'm damned if I'd have been a transvestite.'

Transatlantic call

★ ★

'That's the last thing I do for you. I'm not getting involved any deeper than this.'

Luscious Maria's voice was distant. 'What the hell's the matter with you?'

'That poor girl doesn't deserve what you're doing to her, whatever it is, and, by the way, I don't want to know.'

She hung up. She tried taking her mind off it by leafing through a body-building magazine but Diana Dial's naïve face came between her and the juicy biceps that on other nights tempted her before she fell asleep.

May had found it amusing at first, the idea of teasing a silly little journalist who'd arrived thinking America was paradise. She'd laughed at her Woman Of The World pretensions, her devotion to Julio Iglesias, and her total ignorance. Bit by bit, however, Diana Dial had wormed her way into her heart. And there she was now, stopping her from concentrating on the magnificent attributes of a blond muscleman lifting 500 kilos in one hand.

She had to admit Diana had filled a gap in her life. Since Diana moved into the sauna, May hadn't found getting up in the mornings and the thought of doing things alone nearly so hard. The boredom of the daily grind, and the frustration she felt at other people's indifference, was much more bearable now Diana was around.

Besides, Diana lent her clothes and make-up and wasn't, despite appearances, a miserable prude. She understood her much better than certain others who thought they were liberal.

She'd been right to phone Luscious Maria.

She fell asleep thinking how nice it would be to have Diana beside her, her know-it-all smile and her rather unremarkable body, like a sister you could cuddle up to after a tiring day.

Initiation in the heights

★ ★

Following instructions given her by May, who knew more about this sort of thing, Diana Dial waited for the men Julio Iglesias was sending to pick her up, at a good hotel in Wilshire Boulevard.

'They don't have to know you're living in a sauna,' explained May. 'Though it's nowhere to be ashamed of, mind you.'

So now she was standing on a red carpet covering the pavement, under an awning of the same colour, resisting the insidious glances of a doorman decked out to match.

The international singer's white Mercedes (one of his many cars, including two Rolls Royces, thought Diana), made its appearance at last. She didn't recognize the man at the wheel, but in the back was the press agent, who stuck his head out of the window and smiled.

'We got lost, dammit. Sorry you had to wait.'

The chauffeur rushed round to open the door for her, and Diana did what she'd been wanting to do for the last forty minutes. She went up to the doorman, gave him a dollar bill, and said, 'Here, my good man, get yourself some polish.' And pointed to the brass buttons on his tunic.

Los Angeles is a city that gives you Confidence In Yourself, she thought. *At first you feel lost in its immense acres of asphalt, but the fact you know you're in the land of the winners finally takes over*. True,

81

next to the shining limousines and diamond necklaces grew a weed or two, but that was the price you paid for such a high level of civilization. The memory of the Basque, of the nocturnal decadence of Venice, flashed through her mind and out again as she sunk into the luxurious upholstery of the Mercedes.

For the occasion she was wearing trousers and a bomber jacket of lemon-coloured acrylic which matched her gloves, shoes and a macramé bag she'd made herself a few months earlier following the '*Rumour* Hobbies Suggestions' handbook.

'As you know,' said the press agent, 'Julio has rented an estate in Bel Air, the smartest suburb in Los Angeles.'

Diana nodded.

'He wanted to name his latest record after the house,' the press agent went on, 'that means 1100 Bel Air Place will go down in history. Before Julio rented it, it was just an anonymous mansion, but now thousands of pilgrims from all over the world will visit it. When Julio leaves, its new tenants will have a tough time getting rid of sightseers.'

With her bag (in which, delicately wrapped in tissues, she carried the hair restorer) clutched on her lap, the young journalist listened to the revelations like a rose glowing in the morning dew.

'Julio must have lots of fans staking out his house. Isn't he afraid?'

'He has an impeccable security operation. He was very panicky when John Lennon was assassinated. He was afraid something similar could happen to him.'

'It would be horrifying!' Just thinking about it made Diana's hair stand on end.

'There are some crazy people about. I remember that not long after his father was kidnapped, when he was back safely, the police arrested a guy prowling round the house in Galicia.'

'Good God!' exclaimed Diana.

'They caught him and tortured him, beat him and the like.'

'Did he confess?'

'Yes. He turned out to be a lifelong fan of Julio's. Totally inoffensive, but a bit of a bore.'

'I thought only women got passionate about Julio,' she commented, astonished.

'Not true. Shit, if you saw the guys that hang around him.'

'We're coming into Westbound,' announced the chauffeur, laconically.

'A very elegant suburb,' pointed out the press agent. 'This is where that maniac ran more than twenty people over the other day. These gringos are completely neurotic. When you're not looking, they get a rifle and bump off several generations. You don't have a car, so if I were you, I'd keep a good eye out. Mind you, being in a crowd is more dangerous than walking alone. It's not exciting unless they kill a whole bunch.'

As the car climbed, the space between the houses grew, and the gardens round them became leafier. The chauffeur stopped in front of a huge iron gate leading to an enormous densely thicketed garden. The press agent showed a card to the uniformed guard and the gate opened.

'Now we are entering paradise,' he said. 'Ever noticed how rich people everywhere build their houses on hilltops? It's a perfect way to demonstrate physically their social status. It reassures them to know that the poor are down below. Are you a Marxist?'

Diana played with the zip of her bag. 'Not really. I prefer Chaplin.'

He looked at her puzzled and she quickly changed the subject (had she made A False Move?), asking the names of the nearby trees.

'Palm trees,' replied the press agent, even more puzzled. 'I thought you had those in the Mediterranean.'

'Yes, but they're different. Shorter.'

The car went up and up, and the garden seemed endless. Now and again, hidden among the green, was the unpolluted façade of a grand mansion.

'And this is where the famous stars live?' she asked.

'Only the most elegant. You know how bloody stratified the world of Hollywood is. Living on Sunset isn't the same as Beverly

83

Hills and, of course, only the *crème de la crème* live in Bel Air. The privileged class.'

They were still climbing and the valley, down below, seemed covered by a light layer of mist.

'Typical of the city's pollution,' her escort told her. 'As you can see, it lies between the mountains and the ocean, and there's not much ventilation. Hey, here we are.'

Another gate and another guard, carrying a big gun and a walkie-talkie. He smiled broadly at them. The chauffeur parked the car next to others so splendid the Mercedes looked like a runabout.

'How beautiful!' she exclaimed.

And it was. The house looked like a Swiss chalet, with an abundance of wood and a slate roof dotted with chimneys, lightning conductors and TV aerials. They walked across the garden, up some steps to a terrace, which in turn gave on to a large living-room with glass walls.

'Come on. Got a tape recorder?'

'A midget one,' she said proudly. 'Can I use it?'

'Not a chance. Nor a notepad, or a pencil, nothing. He's invited you to lunch, not an interview. Afterwards you can write a résumé of what he says. But careful, I'll be around to see it's correct.'

They walked across the terrace. Diana stopped in wonderment. A few metres below, the kidney-shaped pool twinkled in the sun. Her heart stopped: a slim bronzed figure was swimming back and forth underwater, in impeccable champion style.

'Oh, it's Him!' gasped Diana.

She also spotted Dr Iglesias, in flowery swimming-trunks, arms crossed, standing barefoot on the grass by a couple of men she didn't know and a beautiful blonde, lounging languidly in a deck-chair, talking down a cordless phone.

A pang of jealousy gripped her breast. Was this young unknown her idol's New Love? Was she, Diana Dial, about to uncover the secret romance of the world's most sought-after bachelor?

'Hi,' said Julio breaking the surface like a dolphin, and Diana had to hold the rail to stop herself fainting. 'How are you? Excuse me a minute, but I have to do some underwater exercises. My doctor says they strengthen the lungs. I do them every day.'

She stood there in a daze until the press agent shook her arm.

'Let's go in,' he said. 'Julio doesn't like people seeing him in bathing-trunks.'

She recalled rumours that one of his legs was thinner than the other, a result of the unfortunate childhood accident that made him Give Up Football and Take Up Singing. But so what? Each of Julio's legs was perfect, in its own way.

In the lounge was a group of people Diana already knew, either because Fernán had already introduced her, or because they were always in magazines, like Tony Rennis, composer of some of Julio's songs, or Albert Hammond, who'd written 'To all the girls I've loved before' for him. She looked around for Ramón Arcusa, who produced his records, but was told he was busy on the new album.

Although she was teetotal, Diana Dial would gladly have had a drink to celebrate her entry into Julio's Inner Circle, but no one offered her one. They all had their noses in newspapers and magazines.

'Have you read *US Today?*' asked the press agent.

'Of course. Wonderful article, isn't it?'

'Not bad. But it's fucking annoying that Roger & Cowan take the credit for having launched Julio in the US. All those guys do is make money out of the stars on their books. They get them along to a party, invite the press, then send the bill. The only thing they have that's worth anything is their address book. They didn't even get Julio on the cover of *People* yet.'

'I read somewhere,' said Diana, presumptuously, 'that they're the best image-makers. They made Rita Hayworth and Kirk Douglas.'

'Yes, but now they concentrate on making money, and that's it. If you're not careful, they make total fools of you. On Julio's birthday, they sent over a bottle of Moët et Chandon. All the press photographers snapped Julio making a toast, of course. Can you believe they not only sent us a bill, but also invoiced the champagne company, and the makers of the watch on Julio's wrist?'

'What a cheek,' sympathized Diana.

'It's not that bad,' joined in Ray, the manager, who'd been silent up till then. 'They do a good job.'

Albert Hammond looked up from *Billboard* at Diana. 'You're Spanish, aren't you? Pretty jealous lot. I was there in the Sixties. They could've had a star in me, but they couldn't see it. Now I've made it in the States.'

Diana said nothing, impressed. *It's true*, she thought, *there's a lot of injustice in the world.*

At that moment, Julio Iglesias made his entrance. He wore a long towel round his waist, his irresistible torso bare, and his wet shiny hair combed back.

'You!' he exclaimed, pointing to the journalist with his forefinger, like Robert de Niro in his best films. 'You're Diana Dial.'

Diana nodded as she got up, overcome by emotion, and, impelled by some Strange Inner Force, she threw herself in his arms.

Julio kissed her on both cheeks.

'I'm Curro,' interrupted a squat little man who'd come in with Julio and Dr Iglesias.

'She's my son's number-one fan. You should have seen her the other night at the concert. The tension, the emotion. What is it you do, dear? A journalist, aren't you? You stick with my son. All the journalists who have do very well.'

'Papa, don't start all that again,' admonished Julio, rolling his eyes. 'Anything new about me?' He turned to the others.

'It's all wonderful,' they chorused.

'What do they say, what do they say?'

They gave him a rundown.

'Fine, well, I'll get dressed and we'll have lunch. All Spanish, we only eat Spanish here.' He smiled a devastating smile just for Diana. 'Isn't this better, an informal relaxed lunch, rather than a rigid interview? In the simplicity of my private life, you'll see what I'm like.'

'I'll see what he's like,' repeated Diana to herself, determined not to forget a single word her idol pronounced during lunch.

The singer was away for a few minutes that to Diana seemed like centuries, and when he came back, dressed like Robert Redford playing cricket on a university campus, they all went into the dining-room. Well, not all of them. To her amazement, all the employees traipsed off to the kitchen. *It's normal*, thought Diana, *only the chosen few can eat with a genius.*

And she was one of the chosen. She sat on Julio's left, on the doctor's right. Under the exquisite linen tablecloth (at least that's what it seemed), she crossed her fingers. She knew she was living a Never To Be Repeated Moment. A girl with dark skin and a sweet smile, and a South American accent, served the wine in willowy glasses. Diana was surprised at the size of the bottle, about the same size as a six-year-old fed on a year's UNICEF quota.

'You'll have never have tasted a better wine than this,' observed Julio.

'Nothing but the best for our star,' said the man called Curro.

Diana was surprised to see a wine merchant sitting at table, but she soon forgot, fascinated by the label of the bottle Julio was waving in front of her nose. *What a terribly, terribly French name*, she mused; but she knew she'd never remember it, since she wasn't very good at languages.

The happiness that flooded Diana Dial's heart ebbed somewhat as the girl whom she'd seen in the garden came and sat on Julio's right. Her skin was apricot, her eyes like two crystal beads and her hair a golden waterfall to her waist.

'May I introduce my girlfriend?' laughed Julio.

Several questions rushed into Diana's mind. Was it a Really Serious affair? Had the singer already forgotten Isabel, the wife whom history had proved totally unworthy of him? What would Chabeli, his beloved daughter, think of this? And, first and foremost, why the hell did Julio like such young, insipid girls? Even all the advances in plastic surgery by Dr Pitengy (who'd worked such miracles with Gina Lollobrigida and Ira de Fürstenberg) couldn't for a single moment make it possible for Diana

87

Dial to attract Julio, she thought in desperation.

And if this wasn't possible, was Life Worth Living? With a superhuman effort and a good gulp of wine, she got a grip on herself. At the end of the day, her task was to be present at events and bear witness to them. A journalist must not take sides, must not get involved. Viceversa had drummed that into her. Or rather, Viceversa said the opposite, but she understood what he meant. Suddenly she felt an acute nostalgia for Barcelona, the magazine, and above all, her boss, who'd protected her at the worst turning-point of her life and who now trusted her. *If he were here, he wouldn't let me be upset by a synthetic blonde beside my idol.* And she decided to be worthy of Viceversa for what was left of the lunch, and keep her grief bottled up inside.

'Do you like the gazpacho?' asked Julio. 'All the ingredients are from Spain.'

She couldn't care less. She only had ears from him and eyes for the stupid hand caressing his neighbour's thigh.

'So tell me, how are things in Spain?' asked the singer. 'Do they still doubt my international success?'

'They're awful,' butted in Albert Hammond. 'Really awful.'

'Oh, no,' Diana jumped to her compatriots' defence. 'They're just ignorant. They haven't been lucky enough to see with their own eyes, like I have.'

A deep pleat of gloom furrowed the singer's brow, and this — the fact that his brow was so wide and the furrow so deep — reminded Diana of Mission Hair Restorer, although she decided to keep the subject for later. She knew she couldn't humiliate Julio in public by talking about his premature baldness.

'It's all the fault of you journalists,' said Dr Iglesias. 'My son should be on the front page every day now he's such a hit abroad.'

Diana agreed. How much better than letting all those wars, coups, bombs, and the rise in the cost of living, grab the best newspaper slots.

'Luckily,' went on the charming gynaecologist to the Madrid upper classes, 'the Americans have realized how brilliant my Julio is.'

'The thing is, Papa,' said the singer, 'you've seen how they treat stars here, no matter how old they are. Here, once you've made it, you're always somebody.'

He put his spoon on his plate and gestured towards the window, without, to Diana's mortification, letting go of the siren's thigh.

'Look at this land, Diana,' he said.

She obeyed, enraptured, like the end of those Cine-club films that Tender Titi had made her watch before he went bananas over El Puma. 'This'll educate you a bit,' he used to say. Well, anyway, just like the last reel of those films where the farmer, having struggled courageously against the elements to save his property for an hour and a half, looks towards the horizon with tears in his eyes, Julio Iglesias fixed his gaze on the Californian hills like someone who'd just reached the summit of the world.

'Look at this land,' he repeated, 'and tell me if it isn't blessed. You plant any old thing, and it grows overnight. All you have to do is pick the fruit. You know, Diana, Europe has grown old. Our civilization is outdated. Now you see goats in Granada, and camels shit at the foot of the pyramids with no consideration at all.'

Seduced by the melodious sound of His Voice, the journalist knew America and Julio were all she desired. The genius was right. It wasn't just a change of scenery. There was something else: the need to be reborn amid acres of vineyards, fields of corn like in *Superman (The Movie)*, skyscrapers of steel and glass, and golden youths with jaws sculpted by chewing-gum. This was the real America, not the filth of Venice or the corpses May went on about.

'Besides, you can't live in Spain these days.' Dr Iglesias shook her from her reverie.

'Why not?'

'What d'you mean, why not? Have you forgotten I was kidnapped? D'you think I can be comfortable in a country where I need bodyguards? I was on the far right, now I'm on the liberal right; that is, I don't care what individuals think, as long as the people in power think like me. But it's not right that an illiterate worker has the same right to vote as a doctor. Don't you agree?'

Diana was about to be evasive (she never knew what to say when people talked politics at her), but Julio came to her rescue.

'Papa, don't start all that again. As I was saying, Diana, when will the Spanish start appreciating the good things they have, admiring artists like Plácido Domingo or Severiano Ballesteros, or me, if you like, we who carry our country's name beyond our own borders?'

Deeply moved, Diana Dial promised herself she'd do everything in her power to remedy this intolerable state of affairs.

They'd reached the coffee without her realizing, and Julio got up, followed by the young blonde.

'Time to leave. I've got to go to the recording studio, but before that I need my siesta.'

Siesta! With another woman. Diana overcame her pain and, on an impulse, opened her bag, took out the bottle of hair restorer, slipped it into the singer's jacket pocket, and as she kissed his perfumed cheek, she whispered some advice:

'Rub this liquid vigorously into your scalp after shampooing. The results are spectacular.'

The traitor

★ ★

The chauffeur drove in silence (the press agent had stayed at the house) and Diana was deep in thought.

'Shall I take you to the hotel?'

She nodded, though it'd be awful to have to face the doorman again, she thought.

The pink Los Angeles dusk was settling on the valley. As if in a dream, Diana watched herself leaving Bel Air in the Mercedes, and in the distance the lights of the city spread out like a carpet, twinkling on one by one.

'Has your magazine got money?'

She didn't understand the question, and made him repeat it.

'Well, can't complain,' she boasted. 'Why?'

'No reason.'

The chauffeur shut his trap again, and kept it shut till they got to Westbound. Then, unexpectedly, he took off his cap, put it on the passenger seat and scratched his neck.

'Been to the Chinese Theatre? Want to go?'

Diana was irritated. 'I really don't want to go to the theatre.' She was dying to tell May about her meeting with Julio.

The chauffeur shrugged. 'I thought you'd like to see the footprints of Hollywood's greatest stars on the pavement outside.'

May hadn't shown her that yet. 'OK,' she accepted. 'But just a quick look.'

Two hours later, loaded down with various film stars' biographies, Jackie Collins's latest best-seller, that photo of Marlon Brando in a vest, and two dozen key-rings commemorating the Los Angeles Olympics, Diana Dial was eating a magenta-coloured ice-cream with Julio Iglesias's chauffeur, whose name turned out to be Lucas and who had opened her eyes to the delights of myth-buying on Hollywood Boulevard.

The biggest thrill, apart from shopping – normally Diana's maximum pleasure –had been seeing close up the famous stars with the artists' handprints, footprints and signatures in cement. All the same, it was a bit pathetic seeing tourists eating ketchup-smothered hamburgers and french fries as they trampled on the venerable relics of Clark Gable, Vivien Leigh or Charlton Heston, and sometimes the tomato even dripped on to the sacred insignia. But Diana had by now absorbed enough of the Californian spirit to know that all that was part of the same, unique and indissoluble heritage.

You can't have roses without thorns, as Viceversa would say.

Lucas had proved attentive, although somewhat stiff, escort. And, needless to say, mysterious. When Diana, drunk with Hollywooditis, had commented, 'Julio's star will be on the pavement one day,' Lucas had murmured something nondescript and merely shrugged his shoulders, instead of indulging in the expressive show of unswerving loyalty Diana expected.

None the less, he was someone who actually worked for Julio, and she couldn't get over that.

'Please call me Diana,' she conceded, after savouring the first spoonful of ice-cream.

What did it matter if he was only a common chauffeur? After all, he wasn't black, so she was spared having to remember the attitudes adopted by characters in Sidney Poitier films.

Lucas was from Almería, he'd told her that before; he was thirty-something and had a brilliant smile. Diana couldn't avoid mentioning his beautiful teeth, and he said he owed it all to Julio Iglesias.

'He can't bear anyone in his entourage with bad teeth. He packs you off bloody quick to get them capped or something.'

So good to his servants, thought Diana. One more charm to add to the singer's many-faceted personality.

'Have you been with him long?' she asked.

'About five years. But I'm leaving.'

'Why?'

Lucas made a vague gesture. 'I want to branch out, start a tapas bar here in Hollywood, with Spanish omelette, paella, pan con tomate, chorizo, things which attract tourists. My wife's Catalan, she's a brilliant cook, and has a good nose for business. We should do well.' He stared into the distance dreaming.

'If I worked for Julio, I'd never leave him,' said Diana.

'All that glitters isn't gold.'

Diana stared at him, incredulous.

'I could tell you a few things,' added Lucas. 'If I did, of course, I'd like to get a decent price.'

The light was beginning to dawn on Diana. 'You mean you'd betray *Him* for a fistful of miserable pesetas?'

'I'd rather be paid in dollars.'

She stood up, shocked. 'I'm not listening to this, *my man*.' She emphasized '*my man*' because these things put people in their place.

Unfortunately for Diana, as she stood up she knocked over her ice-cream and a repulsive big blob spread over the leg of her impeccable lemon-coloured trousers.

'Seltzer!' ordered the traitorous Lucas gallantly.

'I don't need your help,' snapped Diana, whipping away the jar the waiter was holding out to him. She rubbed the sartorial disaster, but she was so nervous she only managed to spread the stain.

'Come on, I'll take you home,' said Lucas, holding her arm.

She got in the car, slammed the door and sank into a sulky silence.

'Pity you're so virtuous.' He looked at her disdainfully in the rear mirror. He opened the glove compartment and took out half a dozen cassettes. 'These mean money. For you and me.'

93

Suddenly he swung the wheel, drove up a deserted side street, put his foot on the brake then turned to Diana.

'This Mercedes has collapsible seats,' he announced.

No sooner said than done. His went down, and Diana found herself with Lucas from Almería alongside pawing her tits.

'My wife's flatter than the map of a mirror.'

Diana began to tremble. She knew it was useless to scream.

'Come on, kid. You persuade your boss and we'll share the loot from my memoirs.'

The young journalist gathered enough presence of mind to pronounce the phrase which saved her honour: 'In the name of the magazine *Rumour*, kindly take your hands off me, or I'll call a policeman.'

Lucas looked at her, thought it over, silently pushed the button again, and his seat went back up. He started the car.

'If I go to *Hola!* with the exclusive, they'll pay what I ask.'

'Ha!' laughed Diana, rather hysterically. 'No Spanish magazine, d'you hear, not a single one, will dare publish lies like that about a singer loved by decent people of the world.'

That apparently made Lucas think. Finally, he conceded. 'All right, I'll take pesetas.'

'Not pesetas, nor piss-eaters. And where the hell are you taking me?'

'The Sheikh's Delights sauna, sweetheart. One of the worst dives in the whole of Los Angeles. I've a friend in the police, and he took the trouble of checking the phone number you gave us.'

Diana blushed. *Bloody meddler!*

'Calm down, kid, I haven't told anyone. It'll be our secret.'

'My magazine can easily afford a five-star hotel for me,' she replied, haughtily, 'but everything was full because of the Games and . . . ' She stopped. She didn't have to explain anything to a wretch like him.

'In those tapes,' he said, pointing to them, 'you'll find lots of things that will interest you. Julio's secrets. Enough to tempt readers with for weeks. It'd be a fantastic scoop for you.'

'I don't bargain with my honour,' Diana cut him short.

Lucas shrugged. 'So, I suppose you're not even interested in what happened with Diana Ross when he pinched her bum.'

'What! Pinched her bum! He may be a bit of a rogue but he's also a gentleman.'

'Gentleman? With this?' Lucas made a rude gesture with the middle finger of his right hand. 'If you knew what he thinks of women . . .'

'Shut up! Shut up!' moaned Diana Dial.

Luckily, they'd arrived at the Sheikh's Delights. Lucas stopped the car and the young journalist alighted regally before the chauffeur had time to open the door. On the pavement, Diana faced him defiantly.

'I never want to see you again.'

'Seriously, don't you want to know what Ross's reaction was?'

'No! And if you go ahead with your despicable scheme, I'll denounce you. I'll tell Julio the kind of wretched, vile, treacherous individual he has driving his wonderful cars.'

Lucas smiled. 'Impossible, sweetheart. Despite that twee look of yours, as if butter wouldn't melt in your mouth, I can tell you'd never do the dirty on a working-class lad.'

Diana snorted, exasperated, and looked round for help. The neighbourhood transvestites and prostitutes were busy with other things. Lucas took advantage of this momentary hesitation to slip the tapes in her bag.

'Listen to them in bed,' he smiled cynically, 'you won't regret it.'

She was going to hit him with her bag and throw the tapes back at him, but her avid journalist instinct got the better of her. She turned and walked jauntily towards the sauna, its fluorscent lights twinkling lewdly on the front. As she opened the door, Lucas's voice shouted behind her.

'What Ross said was that if he touched her again, she'd send the Jackson brothers to rough him up.' And he burst into a revolting laugh.

Bloody liar, said Diana to herself, livid.

Flop was at the reception desk, in his usual state of collapse. He opened one eye.

'Anything wrong?' he asked.

Diana looked at him. 'Did you know that being a journalist is the second most dangerous profession in the world?'

'What's the first?' Flop opened the other eye.

'A sauna receptionist who sticks his nose into things that don't concern him.'

★ ★

Flop told her that May was out buying clothes in an auction at one of the Studios, so Diana went straight up to her room. She shed her lemon-yellow outfit and took a shower, which scraped her skin like a frogman's embrace. Then she got into bed, completely naked, enjoying the feel of the sheets.

She lit a cigarette as she examined the tapes. She knew the sensible thing to do would be to throw them away, but she couldn't resist the temptation of putting one, any one, in the cassette player May had lent her. Lucas's voice suddenly filled the room, and Diana felt guiltier than Cain trying to make a key-ring from the jawbone, under God's enquiring gaze.

'When I entered Julio Igelsias's service, I thought his was a normal family.'

Hell, thought Diana, *that bodes ill*.

'But I soon discovered that was just appearance. What appeared in magazines, the smiling father and mother, Julio always the victim, that was just a façade.'

She pushed the eject button and put in another tape.

'None of the people working for Iglesias, including his most trusted employees, feels the least bit secure. Julio can sack them from one day to the next; for a tantrum, a fit of pride or because now he's bound hand and feet to CBS.'

Suffering pangs of conscience, Diana went on listening.

'CBS don't like the Spanish clique round Julio Iglesias. They want to put him in the hands of their experts. They never miss an opportunity to humiliate the Spaniards. After one of his latest concerts in Los Angeles, the record company organized a party in honour of their associates from Japan, who were on a visit. Well, they only let Julio in. His entourage would have stayed outside if Alfredo Fraile hadn't had it out with the Yanks. Mind you, one day they're going to sack Alfredo too, or Julio himself will make things so difficult his manager will pack it in. Besides, things aren't the same for him since Carlos Iglesias took over the economic side of things and his eagle eye controls everything.'

Carlos Iglesias! The illustrious breast surgeon, the man who gave up operating on countesses' boobs and sacrificed his all for his beloved brother!

'Not even his secretary,' went on the wretched Lucas, 'his most faithful servant, can be sure he won't be fired overnight. He himself may leave after a quarrel, but he always comes back. He's content if he can drink beer behind his master's back, while he vicariously enjoys the luxury around him. He gets in a panic over choosing which suit the singer will wear, examining his shirts, setting out his underwear. Though he has to eat in the kitchen, he likes the life, he likes automatic cars and American houses. After all, when the boss gave him the job, he was selling shoes. His handball career was over.

'Another one walking a tightrope since the Americans took over is his press agent. Last summer he almost got the boot because he gave the best photo of Julio in Paris to a convent school magazine. But I'm sure nothing escapes him, he even takes notes, and any day now he'll hang his master's dirty clothes in public.'

Look who's talking! Diana was shocked. But went on listening.

'He's Colombian, from Popayán. Apparently his father was the warden of the prison there. Popayán is a city flattened by earthquakes every so often, and it has given Colombia fourteen presidents and Julio Iglesias a press agent. Must be a record. He was a journalist when he met Julio, and even flirted with Communism. The great man obviously converted him to Capitalism without too much effort, and now shows off about having a leftie in his group.'

Diana paused. Would Lucas from Almería have another copy of the tapes? Of course he would. So getting rid of them would be no use. She went on listening.

'Julio only likes fawners and flatterers. Like Curro, a squat little bloke with glasses, a Mexican. He's a serious mythomane. His family had the biggest mattress business in Mexico, but when his parents died he asked for his share of the fortune and began spending it on the good life. He collects famous people as others collect butterflies or pocket watches. He used to have a wife who went everywhere in black crêpe, flanked by two pooftas playing the fool for her. Poor old Curro hovers round the stars on his own now. He's a friend of Cantinflas and is always hanging round Julio, on the pretext of keeping his cellar well stocked. Julio uses him, like he does everybody.'

This was nauseating, and endless. Still, she felt so comfy in bed . . .

'Albert Hammond and Tony Rennis suck up to him too, it's only natural. They're getting rich on royalties from the songs they write for him. Hammond grew up in Gibraltar, but goes round saying he's a Londoner. He hates the Spanish, because when he landed in Spain no one took any bloody notice. He doesn't miss a single chance to stir up trouble on the subject.'

Julio wouldn't allow it! No singer is as patriotic as he is, he takes every opportunity to fly the red and gold flag in his concerts round the world.

'Julio hasn't a single peseta invested in Spain. If he is ever sued and loses, they'll have to impound his royalties. And apparently he doesn't even have Spanish nationality, but Panamanian; it was given him by Omar Torrijos's brother, who was a friend of his, though this can never be proved. I've tried to get a look at his passport thousands of times, but Alfredo Fraile's secretary guards it like gold-dust.'

Anyway, thought Diana, Julio's patriotism is all inside him. He doesn't own anything in Spain, not even a house, because he knows all Spanish homes consider him part of the family, and he carries them round with him in his heart.

'It irritates him that they don't pay enough attention to him in Spain. Every time he pees he wants to be on a cover, and he'd be thrilled to bits if they named him "favourite son", or decorated him, or anything like that. At his home in Miami, he gets all the gossip magazines (those he reads) and the newspapers, though he only leafs through ABC. When they publish anything unfavourable, his manager has to hide it so he doesn't get depressed.'

Depressions? wondered Diana. *It's the price of fame*, she told herself. The price of the purple, as the Romans said to Nero. Had Julio really forgotten how to live, as one of his most beautiful and successful songs suggested? Could he still be pining for Isabel? Had all his fame, all his fortune, not let him forget his disappointment in love? Diana felt she wanted to take the singer in her arms and cuddle him like a baby.

'Then there's Alvaro, the photographer. He never knows if Julio's going to keep him on or not. He's a really nice guy, but his name's Rodríguez, and what Julio would like is to take David Hamilton around with him. Of course, someone like that wouldn't put up with Julio's whims and foibles. Even José Maria Castellví couldn't stand it and he was the one, as far as I know, who created Julio's image and taught him how to pose and dress. They ended up at daggers drawn. After seven years working together, Castellví left with the clothes he stood up in and a plane ticket bought with money Alfredo lent him. Apparently they didn't even send him his things. They kept his car and his clothes went to the secretary who was the same size.'

What a nerve, this Lucas. Diana put in a new tape.

'His mother couldn't get over having been left by Dr Iglesias. He, meanwhile, was having a ball, which Julio thought was fine because he likes men to enjoy themselves. His father nearly bought a flat in Rio de Janeiro, paid for by his son of course, but he got tired of the girl he had there. In the meantime, his mother, who is very Catholic, suffered terribly and kept making scenes.'

Diana pushed the fast-forward impatiently.

' . . . his mother can't stand Isabel. She says she tricked her son. As for Julio, he doesn't even want her name mentioned, he uses a disdainful tone when he talks to her on the phone, and more than once I've heard him refuse her permission to take the children somewhere or other.'

Inconceivable! Isabel, that wonderful woman, with whom at times Diana completely identified. She had just a bit too much bum, and a bit too little cunning, to be like her. The rest she could do with make-up.

'As for his children . . .'

Ah, no! Not that! Diana Dial was not prepared to let Lucas touch them, those Poor Innocent Children. She did what she should have done at the beginning. She put the tapes in a plastic bag, got off the bed, and suddenly realized that the curtain of the street-level window weren't drawn, that she was starkers, and that a black guy as big as a Harlem Globetrotter was wanking off with a look on his face like a character in a post-war Spanish film gazing at the Virgin of Fátima. Diana backed away, drew the curtains, put on her robe (a quilted Never Copulate model), and left her room carrying the bag.

She crossed the hallway, opened one of sauna rooms and, ignoring the couple (she didn't notice the sex, although she could imagine) having it off on the bench, went over to the stove and threw the tapes on.

Honestly, how could Julio trust people like that? How much better for the singer to confide his secrets in someone like her.

Diana Dial never gave up. Diana Dial would defend her idol to the very last. To the death!

She went back to her room more resolute than ever. She drew the curtains back. The black guy was still there, his flies half-zipped and his eyes bleary. She took her time taking off her robe. Then she shook her hair like a Thirties screen goddess and, when the guy put his hand down below for a second session, closed the curtains again. *Bloody hell, the things people do for fun*! She would never understand this country. So advanced in some things, so barbaric in others.

The astrological chart

★ ★

The day after her enchanting lunch with Julio Iglesias (and the confrontation, with his chauffeur, followed by the heroic decision not to listen to his memoirs), Diana Dial was dumbfounded to see a strange advert in the showbiz pages of the *Los Angeles Times*. It was a small announcement and she probably wouldn't have noticed it had it not been just below a review (favourable, of course) of the concerts with which the Spanish singer was still bewitching the Californian city. It went as follows:

ASTROLOGICAL CHARTS — SALADINO & MABEL LOOK
INTO THE FUTURE AND THE MOST SECRET ASPECTS OF
YOUR PERSONALITY, ARE YOU INTERESTED IN MORE
THAN *RUMOUR*? IF THE EYES DON'T SEE, TO THE
HEART LOVE REMAINS A *RUMOUR*. FOR DIANA, GOD-
DESS WHO MAKES SENSE OF *RUMOUR*, DIAL 565 3712,
HOLLYWOOD, LOS ANGELES.

Heavens, thought Diana, it was obviously a coded message. It was written in Spanish, the word *Rumour* (Her Magazine) was underlined three times, and it mentioned her *nom de guerre*, albeit disguised. Diana Dial's relentlessly deductive mind deduced the deducible: A Message For Her. The author was, of course, Ignacio Clavé. Unless it was written by the dog.

She picked up the phone and began to dial, but the international spy she'd suddenly become thought twice: TV heroes in similar situations always call from phone booths. She went outside. Luckily, there was a phone between the launderette and the shop selling false fingernails.

As she was leaving the Sheikh's Delights, she bumped into May, who was beginning her working day with a long lanky client. That morning the sauna was truly bubbling, not just from the steam filtering mischievously from the private booths but because everyone was celebrating the victory of various American athletes. Diana couldn't get very worked up about sport at the best of times, even less now she had Transcendental Matters to think about.

'I thought you'd never call,' said Ignacio Clavé's voice at the other end of the line. 'I've put that advert in three days running. Cost me an arm and a leg. Good thing I finally thought of putting it under something about Julio. I should've known it's the only thing you read. You'll always be an ignoramus.'

Ignoramus, her! With all she'd learned about Life recently.

'Get over here quick,' he gave her an address, 'and don't tell a soul you're coming to see me, *not a soul*,' he insisted, emphatically.

The address Clavé had given her was relatively near the sauna. That is, only nine dollars by taxi, which in a city like Los Angeles wasn't a fortune. Diana usually enjoyed the company of Los Angeles taxi drivers. They were polite, opened the door when you got in and out, let you smoke, emptied the ashtray before driving off, and occasionally even invited you for a Coke or Pepsi, usually a diet one, because they compensated for their job's lack of exercise by cutting down on calories. The only black mark against them was their exasperating tendency to get lost, although that was understandable given the city's size and geographic complexity. On those occasions, the driver smiled courteously, stopped the metre and hauled out from the depths of his glove compartment a street map the size of a telephone book.

Diana was usually thankful for these interludes: they gave her time to find out all about her driver's private life, and at the same time let her practise the language of Harold Robbins with someone who had no choice but be friendly since he was being paid. But that particular morning, down Fountain Street between Fuller and Poinsettia, she couldn't help being annoyed when the driver stopped the cab and got out his familiar mammoth map.

She listened absentmindedly to her driver's explanation. It was quite obvious Ignacio Clavé needed her urgently. Why would he have come so far otherwise? He who, as he was so fond of saying, only liked travelling via the stars. 'The important thing is to have an open mind, to meet people,' he'd say. 'Everything there is to learn is within us.' Of course this spiritual side of her colleague contrasted with the recent, for her, discovery of his commercial inventor spirit.

They finally set off again and the driver left her opposite a narrow passage in the middle of a block of one-storey houses, each with a little garden and a white picket fence round it. Diana found the number she wanted was down the alleyway that separated the row of prefabricated dwellings, which looked like icing sugar. The vegetation was overwhelming but not particularly exotic, just a gigantic version of the botanical gardens in any halfway sunny city.

The door behind which she supposed she'd find Ignacio was half-hidden by two such extraordinary examples of fern that Diana felt like saying hello and asking after their mother.

Ignacio himself opened the door. He greeted her with, 'You've come at a bad time.'

What Diana saw then, not in this order, but in terms of the impression they made on her, was: an amazingly tall man lying on the floor of a room furnished with a small couch, a television and two videos (all on); a work table and a chart on the wall behind it; Mabel with half her mane orange and the other half a bilious green, sitting on the man's chest vigorously licking his cheeks; a dark-haired man with green eyes, in Bermudas, his torso bare, holding a piece of cloth soaked in something under the man's nose; and an older man, fit and attractive, reading out loud from a book.

'Amopeyep helup disianisab redundia,' he pronounced, carefully.

'Think it'll work?' asked the younger man.

'It did with Doris Day,' replied the other.

Ignacio took Diana's hand silently and led her into the next room, which turned out to be a bedroom.

'What on earth . . . ?'

'Calm down,' he interrupted. 'What's happening next door is nothing to do with us. Rafa and Guille, whose house this is, are astrologers from Gerona, like me. They've been in California for years. I got in touch with them when I needed a favour. They're just in the middle of a session with Derek.'

'I think I've seen him before.'

'Right. He's the cowboy in the Marlboro advert. Apparently they want to replace him with someone younger, and he's desperate.'

'And they're helping him,' Diana deduced.

'No, they told him the news. They've just read his astrological chart. Now they're trying to bring him round.'

Ignacio studied her thoroughly. 'You look wonderful. More of a tan. More of a woman. More of everything.'

Diana blushed.

'Come here, sit on the bed,' he said.

'Don't try anything.'

'No, but there's nowhere else to sit.'

Diana obeyed, not without a certain reticence. The word *bed* added to the name *Clavé* still gave her the willies. He took her hands.

'Diana, someone is trying to make life difficult for us,' he said, in an intimate tone.

And he told her everything that had happened since they'd last met: the beating, the kidnapping, the rescue, the holiday Viceversa had given him.

'How dreadful. The boss did mention it, but I haven't spoken to him since and I've been so busy.' She stopped, ashamed. To tell the truth, she hadn't given a toss about what had happened to her colleague. 'And what could be the motive behind such a dirty deed?'

Clavé stroked the hairs traversing his head.

'It's obviously something to do with your trip to the States and your friendship with Julio. It's no coincidence that I was kidnapped the day you left. And another thing.'

'What?' asked Diana, in suspense.

'I think you're his real target. Because if what they want is to get to Julio, you're the one who can do it for them.'

'You're talking in the plural,' astutely observed Diana. 'You say only one man attacked you.'

'A gang,' corrected Clavé, rather hurt.

'What makes you think there's more than one?'

'The importance of the prey. If Julio's their target, they can't use only one person. There must be at least twenty of them. Has anything strange, anything odd, happened to you? Has anything alerted your investigative talents, Diana?'

Ignacio had as much confidence in the said talents as in a vegetarian vulture, thought Diana. But she let it pass.

'No, nothing. Everything's gone swimmingly. I went to one of Julio's shows, he invited me to lunch yesterday, I gave him the hair restorer . . . I can't complain.'

Diana told him all that had happened since she'd landed in Los Angeles. The luck she'd had in meeting May. She also explained in glorious Technicolor what kind of a place the Sheikh's Delights was, specially since Ignacio thought she was a prude and she hoped her intense Californian curriculum would change his mind.

'Magnificent.' Ignacio appeared relieved. 'I see you've got around pretty well, despite your inexperience. And how's the book going?'

'Well, that's the most difficult bit. Julio's in such demand, you know. But I'm optimistic.'

'Fantastic. It's time to act. You say you gave him the hair restorer yesterday.'

'Yes. I couldn't do it before. Iberia lost my suitcase with the bottle inside. When they returned it, the bottle was missing, and I had to complain, and . . . '

Ignacio Clavé sprang to his feet.

'What did you say! Heavens above!' he cried, like Enrico Caruso in *The Great Idem*.

'Calm down, I told you I've got it back.'

'Does that mean,' groaned Clavé, '*my invention* was missing for several days? That someone had unhindered access to it.'

'Not *someone*,' said Diana impatiently, 'I told you it was Iberia, Spanish Airlines.'

'Dimwit! You'll always be a dimwit! Don't you realize? What interest can a bottle possibly be to an airline renowned throughout the world for its total disinterest in anything?'

Diana considered this. 'Well, I'll be blowed.'

Ignacio sat down again and made her do the same, holding her wrists tightly. There was not the slightest hint of lust now.

'Tell me everything again, from the beginning. Even things that seem unimportant. There's something fishy going on. Please God I haven't got here too late.'

Back in Europe

★ ★

'Be so good as to keep still.'

'I've got a facial tic.'

'I know, I know. Very unfortunate.'

President Mitterrand tried not to move while the Algerian put the final touches to his make-up. Of all the taxidermists in the world, thought the French President, they had to send me one who was in the FLN. Any day now he'd paralyse him for good.

Drrrriiinnngg. Ahmed picked up the phone.

'It's for you.'

'Well, it wasn't likely to be for you, was it?' growled the President to himself. It was the red phone.

'It's Nancy Reagan. Am I speaking to *chéri* François?'

'Mmmmmm.'

'What's wrong with your voice?'

'I've got my face mask on. What can I do for you? Some more pâté? Another batch of *Marie Claire* stockings? Latest copy of *Nôtre Maison*?'

'No, I've plenty,' replied the First Lady of the other side of the Atlantic. 'But I've got a question about Huuuuuulio.'

'Huuuuuulio? Who's that?'

'You know, the most wonderful singer ever. That boy we all like.'

'Ah, *Julieau!*'

'That's right. He's here in California, you know, and, well, you organized such a lovely birthday party for him last year, I thought you could give me some ideas for a treat. Something *chic*.'

The President's nose itched something terrible and he signalled to Ahmed by looking cross-eyed. Ahmed obediently put a finger in his right nostril and scratched. Mitterrand kept his eyes crossed, and Ahmed stuck it in the left nostril.

'Ah . . . ' sighed Mitterrand.

'What it is, darling?' inquired Nancy.

'Nothing. You know, dear, sometimes being president of a country has its compensations.'

'That's what I tell Ronnie. But it's such a heavy burden . . . '

They got stuck into that theme for a few minutes, until Nancy cut him short.

'Well, what do I do?'

'I can't think of anything offhand. I'll ask the Nightingale of Avignon and let you know.'

'Who's that? An oracle?'

'Good God, woman, no. Our beloved Mireille Mathieu. She's bound to think of something. She's got exquisitely French taste.'

Nancy hung up and Mitterrand lay back again.

'It'll have to be redone. I told you to unplug the phone for our sessions,' spluttered Ahmed.

The president sighed. Bloody Algerians. General Massu was right. The final solution would have been better.

The man who hated multinationals

★ ★

'Where's May?' asked Diana Dial when she got back. A Worrying Doubt had been nagging away at her since her conversation with Ignacio.

'He's taken a couple of days off,' complained Flop. 'Always the same, leaving me in the lurch when I need him most. In the middle of the Olympics, if you please. With everybody on heat.'

'D'you know where I can find her?'

Flop shook his head. 'No idea. When May asks for time off he disappears without trace. Then he comes back a total wreck and I have to look after him. Talking of human debris, some guy wants to see you.'

'Me?'

'Yes; an oddball. He wanted a sauna, nothing else. I hope he showered first. He stank to high heaven.'

Diana's heart missed a beat. It could only be the Basque.

'Where is he?'

'In Number 42. Tell him not to get any ideas. He's not getting it cheap just because he's a friend of yours.'

She left him grumbling away, and went to Number 42 with her stomach in knots. He'd come back, he'd come for her. May was right. Diana knocked on the door feeling Almost A Woman.

'Come in,' said, in Spanish, the voice of the man she'd met in Venice.

Through the steam she made out his body on the bench. He was naked.

'Come here,' he ordered.

Diana didn't hesitate.

'Phew, it's hot,' she commented.

'Take your clothes off.'

She obeyed because the vapour acted as a kind of thin screen between them, and also because she wanted him. Her clothes fell in a heap in a corner. She stood in front of him, he stayed seated.

'Turn around.'

She did. She felt the men's large hands squeeze her buttocks. The pressure was hard, almost unbearable at first, but gradually grew gentler until it was light as a feather. Diana held her breath. Suddenly he put his arms round her waist and held her against him. She was trapped between his thighs and felt his penis harden in the crack.

'You've no idea what being arse-sick is like,' he murmured, his mouth against her back.

He drooled over her skin for a while as he moved her pelvis rhythmically. Then he stood up and, still embracing her, made her bend over the bench, which was just at belly height. He hurt her. It reminded her of the enemas her mother used to give her when she was little, which made her cry from pain and shame. But this time she didn't cry. When you meet A Man Like This, contact like this becomes the Natural Order Of Things.

She did think, however, about life's quirks. And about Viceversa, and how if he found out was happening to her in Los Angeles he'd make her write pornographic serials. But Viceversa must never know. He'd never leave his wife for her if he did.

Not that time either, thought Diana Dial afterwards. Perhaps she would never know the incomparable happiness of A Healthy Sex Life. The Basque lay over her for a while and then stood straight.

'Let's have a shower,' he said abruptly.

They both stood in the little space behind a plastic curtain. Diana anxiously awaited New Experiences Underwater, but the shower passed off as impersonally as if they'd been in the

Underground. When they'd finished, the Basque held out a towel to her and wrapped another round his waist.

'I'm going to get my clothes. I'll wait for you in the street.'

Diana picked up her things and went to her room while he walked off to the changing-rooms. She was disappointed (She Still Did Not Know) but she felt weak at the knees. Suddenly she realized she had to dress pretty sharpish; no drying her hair, or giving it a quick twirl with Beautycurl tongs. If she didn't get her skates on, the guy was liable to disappear off into the blue again. Did she really love him? As much as Viceversa? More than Julio Iglesias? Could a woman love Three At A Time? Of course she could in the City of the Angels.

She came galloping out of the Sheikh's Delights, tucking her shirt into her jeans, and with her sandals flapping. He was on the pavement opposite, leaning against a tree, hands in pockets, the same cynical look that had caught Diana's eye the first time she saw him.

'I can't make you out,' he rapped out at her. 'I can't make you out at all. A journalist who wants to write a book about Julio Iglesias, a gullible little fool who can't tell dope from Lucky Strikes, living in a seedy sauna.'

He took her arm, making her walk at his pace. 'Come on. I know a place near here, with good booze and decent music.'

Night had fallen and the boulevard lights looked pure cinema. So did the two of them. She glanced at him out of the corner of her eye. He was clean and almost smart in a suit that, though it had seen better days, looked great on him, and a white open-necked shirt that showed a bit of his chest. He had a small scar on his neck, and Diana's heart melted. She stroked it with her fingertip.

'A knife-wound?' she asked, concerned.

'A boil. When I was two.'

She shut up.

'It's here,' he said finally, pointing to a kind of cave from which emanated a violet light.

He walked in ahead of her, and this confirmed Diana's initial impression that he wasn't exactly the epitome of refinement.

Well, you had to get used to everything when you're A World Traveller.

She followed him to a table in the corner furthest from the door. There was a big red candle in the middle (the whole club was candle-lit, which to Diana made it mysterious), and glass stains on the worn wood. He ordered a double bourbon and she a vanilla milkshake.

'And to cap it all, she's teetotal.'

Diana said nothing. He shifted in his seat.

'You think I'm dead-beat, a nobody. Well, I am,' he said, dramatically. 'I'm a failure. But you're a hack journalist and, I can imagine, write for the gutter press. Does Julio Iglesias pay you to publish the rubbish he chooses?' Diana opened her mouth but he didn't let her speak. 'Since I first set eyes on you, I've thought of nothing else.'

That sounded much better than the music they were playing in the club, weird music with words she couldn't quite make out.

'What's this record?' she asked, embarrassed.

'The Fugs. A Sixties group. "I want a girl who can make love like an angel, cook like the devil, move like a dancer, work like a horse, dream like a poet, flow like a stream." Like it?'

'I don't know.' She liked him saying it, but she daren't tell him.

'They don't make music like that any more. And only poor devils like us remember it.'

He downed his drink and ordered another double.

'I'm not ashamed, you know.'

'No reason you should be.' Diana was moved.

'Shut up, dammit. Just shut up. You lot always know what to say. You're always talking. Or rather, writing. Writing lies, so your readers think they're living in the best of all possible worlds. I know you.'

He'd lost his tenderness. Diana looked at him, horrified.

'Now you're going to let me talk. I'll tell you why Julio Iglesias is a success in the States, why a multinational invests seven or eight thousand million to promote an artist who's got no voice and sings the same song he sang when he won in Benidorm, someone who's even past his peak.'

That gave Diana her breath back. Spurred on by indignation, she leapt to the defence of her idol.

'I think Julio's the best.'

'You and lots of others. Haven't you read *Time* magazine? There's a brilliant article in it. They call him the menopause heart-throb.'

'I'm only thirty-two!' yelled Diana. How could she have ever thought she loved him?

'But Operation Julio Iglesias is much more important than all that,' he went on, taking no notice of her. 'What d'you think a multinational is? A convent for the Sisters of Mercy? A place where the best man wins? Don't make me laugh. It's a form of control, of power. A system that sells apparently inoffensive products but really disseminates a way of life. Julio Iglesias represents a system of values that the US multinationals want to spread. Or rather a system that has no values, merely slogans.'

'Julio sings about love. That's a feeling that's universal and eternal.' She felt satisfied with her phrase.

'Don't be ridiculous. D'you really think that's what love is? Your Julio's turned feelings into Plasticine for the consumption of people who can't tell the difference between passion and a cuckoo clock.'

He paused, softening his voice when he came back on the attack:

'Love should provoke rebellion, not submission. Love is transgression, not conformity. Love should drive us crazy, make us fight the cunning, obedient and cowardly dwarf we all have inside us. The only thing those songs you find so moving are good for is making us forget love.'

'Anyway, it's not only Julio who sings them.'

'You're right,' he admitted. 'Twenty years ago we thought the sentimental melody was on its way out. Pop music arrived, young people were fed up; we wanted something different . . . The age of sickly sugar seemed to be over. We had rock, and the revival of folk music . . .'

114

He was looking at her, but Diana realized he wasn't seeing her.

'Groups like the Rolling Stones, who didn't stop being yobs, or Zappa and The Mothers of Invention, or the Fugs . . . All the underground scene. It seemed like a miracle that wouldn't end. But it did. It ended. One day someone discovered we could be manipulated as well; they only had to create new idols.'

'I don't see that this had anything to do with Julio Iglesias and his unprecedented success.'

'Well, it does. Because we're back in the same shit we were in before. Know what was going on in the world while Julio was singing in Benidorm in '68? I won't talk about May '68 in France, you've probably never heard of it . . . Right here, in Chicago, the youngsters who supported the new music, the new lifestyle, felt the wrath of the Establishment at the Democratic Convention. The dream of peace and love was shattered. Julio Iglesias, meanwhile, was saying that life goes on the same . . . He was already voting for Ronald Reagan without even knowing it.'

'Julio's the new Frank Sinatra.' Diana brought the conversation back to basics, since the Basque had gone off at a tangent.

'That's not true. And even if it were . . . know who Frank Sinatra is? He's in the Mafia, OK, but worse than that, he owes his success to the standardization of his voice and his image. When you go and see him, you know exactly what you're going to hear. In this country, they sell books that teach you how to write romantic melodies. They have them for mothers, for girlfriends, for wives, and best of all, laments for lost love. They go down really well – Julio Iglesias's favourite pre-cooked dish. A commodity which sells well. Nothing else.'

'That's not so terrible.' *He's just jealous*, she thought. After all, he'd admitted he was a failure. 'We all want to make a lot of money.'

'It's not that it's bad because it's commercial,' the Basque was getting irritated, 'but because it replaces authentic feelings with feelings that only seem real. Because, thanks to Julio and others like him, people can delegate their responsibility for loving, living, being, to those who govern them. It's the triumph of organized degradation. D'you seriously think that cheap playboy represents something real, something worth listening to?'

He scratched his chin, which today was clean and soft.

'The sad thing is that places like Altamont, Woodstock, the Isle of Wight opened up the way for idols like Julio Iglesias. We thought we were building a new world, but we just watched our illusions die. We thought we'd be free, but the big corporations had already bought and packaged our idea. CBS among others.'

'And why were CBS interested in Julio?' asked Diana, arms crossed. 'Why were they, if he's no good?'

'Because each year they examine the lists of the best-selling Hispanic singers in Latin America, and one year they found that Julio Iglesias had sold half a million records in Argentina alone. That's why they bet on him. But I was telling you about Woodstock (have you any idea what it is?) and the death of our dream at the hands of the multinationals.'

'So did you leave your job?' Diana couldn't help asking.

'No. Not straight away, because I was a bastard too. I'd got used to being somebody in this business, living in this country, and living well, driving a nice car and having my doorman tip his cap to me. And because the only thing I know how to do is sell the music other people make.'

He studied the bottom of his glass.

'In fact, I never left.' He looked at her frankly. 'They fired me when they no longer needed me. All I've got left are what I'm standing up in and the den where I was happy with you the other night.'

Again, Diana Dial's heart was torn between indignation and pity.

'Your book, if you write it, will be another pack of lies, another smoke-screen. I'll tell you why CBS is interested in Julio Iglesias, why they offer him million dollar contracts, why Coca-Cola takes him under its wing.'

'Because he's so famous.'

'No. *They*'re the ones who make and unmake the famous. You've still got a lot to learn. They're interested in Julio because he's the Faust of our time.'

Diana thought hard, but couldn't remember anyone of that name.

'He'd sell his soul to the Devil for what he's been promised. He's famous in the States now, but only he knows what he had to do to get it. And only he knows what he's capable of doing so that he doesn't lose that fame. That is his morality.'

'He's a great fighter.' Diana was getting pretty fed up. Anyway, how dare he talk about morality? She was well aware what his was. He'd stuck it up her arse not all that long ago, in the sauna. Fancy him she might, but he was definitely what Viceversa would call 'a negative and depressive spirit'.

'I've seen plenty of people fall,' the Basque went on, tossing his third double whiskey down. 'He'll fall too.'

'I have to go,' muttered Diana, torn between horror and pleasure.

She wasn't sure she'd see him again if she left. 'Besides,' she added, 'what you're saying all seems a bit confused to me.'

'Bully for you. You'll probably go a long way. You'll write your book, Julio will promote it and you'll earn lots of money.'

'Tell me something. If he's so bad, why does everybody like him?'

'That's exactly why. Because the majority always prefers lies. It's more comfortable, you don't have to face yourself. The people who understand that will always hold power. And there'll always be some Latin with a Yankee soul ready to spread Big Brother's message. Your Julio isn't unique, unfortunately, nor is he the last of his kind. But I'll tell you one thing: the Devil always gets Faust in the end. He takes his soul, and everything else to boot. Julio Iglesias has signed his own death warrant. He'll sacrifice all he owns, the people round him, everything. And in the end, when he has nothing more to give, they'll crush him. That's how it's always been. If he doesn't get fucked up by drugs, like most of them.'

'Drugs!' Diana was horrified.

'Don't worry about that. They've other ways of getting rid of him.'

'Like they got rid of you.' Diana couldn't help it, and then She Felt Bad.

'I didn't mean it.' She held his hand but he took it away. 'Please, forgive me.'

'Let's go, I'll take you home.' He got up and left a couple of crumpled bills on the table. Diana wondered how he got the money. 'It's dangerous to walk these streets alone at this time of night.'

They walked to the door of the Sheikh's Delights in silence. Diana's throat tasted sour, as if she'd swallowed a bitter pill.

'You're wrong about Julio. If you knew him, if you saw how charming and elegant he is, you wouldn't say all this. He's one of the few originals left.'

'Hold your horses, love. *You*'re the one of the few originals left.'

He took her face in his hands (like Montgomery Clift in *A Place in the Sun*, thought Diana) and gave her a long deep kiss tasting of alcohol and wood. Diana closed her eyelids and kept them shut a long time, until his lips left hers and the smell escaped. When she opened her eyes he was gone, and this time she was sure it would be for good.

She didn't even know his name, and she couldn't even tell May.

Meanwhile, in Miami . . .

★ ★

Moncho had been told that Miami was the most dangerous city
in the world. That's why he'd come armed with his statutory
flick-knife, which he'd wangled through Barajas airport by
saying it was for trimming his nails. And now he was being
detained in Miami by a spick cop with a vicious look on his face.

'Sorry,' he drawled, 'we only allow firearms.'

Moncho realized that if he wanted to succeed in this place, like
Al Pacino in *Scarface*, he'd have to modernize his methods. He
also realized there was a lot Tender Titi hadn't told him. This
was like Dallas, lawless city. In the bus which took him to 19th
and 4th the driver turned on the radio news, and a shiver ran
down Moncho's spine. The announcer was saying:

'Investigations are continuing into the shocking case of the
nurseries where babies were sexually abused in ways that are
beyond even the most feverish imaginations. The police have
been working on the case non-stop and to date have arrested one
couple, Marco Antonio Nelson Napoleón Dos Santos and Norma
Nadia Garrupini, accused of allowing the infants in their kindergarten to be used for lascivious practices involving big shots in
Dade County after giving them bottles laced with heroin. The
public was particularly revolted by the case of the infant who
sobbed bitterly whenever his mother (in tears) tried to dress him
in the Mickey Mouse underpants he was wearing the day he was

sodomized in a synagogue by an unscrupulous rabbi.'

By the time Moncho got off at Biscayne Boulevard (very near the sea; he couldn't see it, but he sensed its pungent smell in his nostrils), he already had a pretty good idea of the kind of jungle he was up against and he wondered whether he was prepared for it. It's one thing being a macho in Cera Street (near the statue of Santa Eulalia, saint and virgin, who at one time was the patron of Barcelona), and quite another being an international intriguer in the world capital of vice, drugs, crime, score-settling and traffic in dentures for illustrious old fogeys.

His destination was the sixth floor of a not very tall building. He went up in a lift with an individual dressed as Xavier Cugat in *Million-Dollar Mermaid* who made a sullen gesture indicating he should put his cigarette out if he didn't want to end up in the county jail before nightfall. He went up to a door marked 'Amancio Escalario, Artists Agent' and pushed it.

A dark-haired secretary with breasts practically at her eyebrows smiled at him like a piano.

'I want to see Señor Escalario.'

'Do you have an appointment?'

'No, but I wrote to him from Spain, and I'm sure he wants to see me. My name's Moncho, Moncho Expósito, it's about Señor Puma.'

The girl told him to wait and moved her bum about over her legs in a way that vaguely resembled walking. She knocked on a door behind him and went in. She came out a few minutes later.

'Mister Escalario says wait.'

He picked up that day's paper.

'ACCOUNT SETTLED IN CORAL GABLES. GANGSTERS BURST INTO THE HOME OF A MAFIA BOSS AND DISCONNECT ESSENTIAL ELECTRICAL HOUSEHOLD EQUIPMENT, ELECTROCUTING WIFE AND CHILDREN.'

Shit, what kind of place is this?

This Amancio made him wait almost an hour. Moncho threw impatient glances at the girl (he once used to fancy girls like her, though now he considered himself a one-man man), but she took no notice. He cleared his throat, but she still didn't. He went on reading:

'TAXI DRIVER STRANGLED BECAUSE HE REFUSED TO ALLOW HIS DOBERMAN TO HAVE SEX WITH CUSTOMER'S WIFE.'

The phone rang, the girl said, 'Yes, boss,' then she looked at Moncho and told him he could go in. She accompanied him, brushing her hips against him. *They're all the same*, decided Moncho scornfully.

Amancio Escalario had a hairy wart on his right cheek and a sickly Argentine accent you could cut with a knife. Unlike his compatriots, however, he came straight to the point.

'Sit down,' he said, 'and tell me about the matter of life and death that's threatening my client.'

'Well,' hesitated Moncho, who wasn't used to talking in offices with gold records, posters (mostly of El Puma), and locks of hair in small amulets on the walls.

'Well?'

'The person actually under threat of death, and who may be wiped off the map without the slightest trouble, is Julio Iglesias. El Puma's main rival! The man who replaced him in the favours of CBS.'

'You mean that plonker, that unscrupulous bastard, is finally going to get his just desserts?'

'Exactly,' said Moncho. 'And this is the arm that will do it.' he flexed his biceps till they almost burst.

'Go on, go on, tell me,' urged the other.

And Moncho told him: a friend of his had intercepted 'Operation Hair Restorer', a plan to give Iglesias an even more luxuriant mop of hair than El Puma's.

'I'll be damned!' said Escalario, horrified.

Moncho went on: an agent, in the service of the cause, had managed to change the bottle for one containing something much more harmful.

'Brilliant!' applauded Escalario. Moncho: the false hair restorer was now in Julio's possession, and he would be using it any

121

time now. 'But this is wonderful, *ché*!' cheered Escalario. Moncho: and he only hoped El Puma would reward them when everything had turned out well.

'Of course,' said Amancio Escalario, 'but we want results, not promises.'

'You'll be hearing from us in a day or two,' said Moncho, when he saw the other man get to his feet.

'Fantastic, we'll discuss it then.'

'Aren't we signing anything?'

'What for? Don't be crazy, we Argentines and Spaniards are like brothers! This is a gentlemen's agreement. OK?'

Moncho left the office, a bit cross but convinced he couldn't have done any better. Besides, things were different abroad.

The humidity and heat of the street forced him into an air-conditioned taxi. He'd invested all his savings in this trip and he didn't want to arrive at his friends' house dehydrated.

The Plan

★ ★

Diana was too excited to go to sleep, so she decided to go to the sauna club for a while. It was full of men bellowing and drinking beer as usual, and the transvestite standing in for May – a character with hips like a samovar wrapped in an American flag – made her so depressed she chose to go to her room. Those degenerates were celebrating the American team's victory in the Olympics. They stank of sweat and liquor. On her way to her room Diana passed May's door and instinctively knocked as she did when she wanted advice or simply a bit of company.

The door was ajar. May's perfume, dense and tropical, wafted out, creating the illusion that she was inside. Diana put the light on and came back to reality. She felt tired, sad and older.

She sat on the bed. Were the suspicions Ignacio Clavé had put in her mind true? 'Only our boyfriend or girlfriend, or whatever, could have taken the bottle. What if he's substituted tap water to discredit us?' 'But what for?' she'd asked. She had no answer to that question, or so many others, for that matter. Why had May unexpectedly decided to take some days off?

Suddenly, the truth opened a path through her brain like an Easter Parade. Slowly but surely. The walls were bare. The posters of Marilyn and Richard Gere had gone! Diana rushed to the cupboards and opened them. Nothing. The same with the chest of drawers. Except . . . Something was rolling around at the back of one of them.

Diana put her hand in and took out a cylindrical packet wrapped in newspaper. She tore frantically at it. Her vibrator! In a daze, she pushed the button and saw it still had its two speeds and the little red light at the tip, though the batteries were a bit low. With the vibrator was a little piece of paper written hurriedly in an uneducated hand:

'I'M GOING AWAY. FORGIVE ME FOR HURTING YOU. DON'T LET JULIO USE THE HAIR RESTORER. I'LL NEVER FORGET YOU.'

Stunned by the discovery, Diana sat on the bed again and began to cry. She still didn't understand anything. Who was May of the Mountains really? Why was she involved in the conspiracy, and what was the conspiracy, anyway? She was sad, desperately sad, because in one day she'd lost both the Basque and her friend.

She thought of Viceversa. She thought of *Rumour*'s agony column. 'Above all, dear, don't be beaten by adversity. Life has many twists and turns, and when God closes a door, he opens a window.' It was true! Diana Dial Couldn't Give Up. With her comforter in her hand, she dialled Ignacio Clavé's number. After speaking to him, she quickly packed her case.

'I have to leave urgently,' she told Flop. 'Can I have my bill?'

After paying an amount that seemed exorbitant but not worth arguing over (*Rumour* could afford it), Diana rushed over to the house in Fulton in a taxi. They were all there except for the Marlboro fainter, and Diana politely asked how he was.

'Ah, fantastic,' said Rafa absentmindedly. 'As we predicted, they fired him, but he got a job as a cowboy statue in front of the Waxworks on Hollywood Boulevard. He's absolutely delighted.'

Then Diana told them her news.

'We'll have to be careful,' said Ignacio, when she'd finished. 'She's obviously a very intelligent woman who knows what she's hatching. That note may be a trap.'

'Didn't you say it was a man?' asked Guille.

'Well, it's not a man or a woman . . . exactly,' Diana clarified, or rather obscured.

'Has it got tits?' asked Rafa.

'Yes.'

'And a prick?'

'Yes. Very big,' admitted Diana, blushing.

'So,' decided Rafa, 'it's a whale of a transvestite.'

'Whatever,' interrupted Ignacio Clavé, 'we're dealing with a very crafty individual who has been toying with this poor unfortunate girl like a cat with a mouse. Heavens! I wonder what strange uses my foolproof hair lotion has been put to.'

'I'll never be able to think of her in the same way,' whimpered Diana, 'if I ever see her again, that is. I hate her more than Lucas.'

Ignacio shot an urgent look at each one of the group. 'We have to proceed with caution. They mustn't know we're here, and even less that we know what they're up to.'

'But May warned me in her note.'

'Who knows if she wrote it? In any case, the anti-Julio gang don't know that I and my innate talent for investigation are here.'

'I'm glad you've come,' murmured Diana, looking gratefully at Clavé. 'In moments like these, a girl appreciates a good man.'

In the astrologer's living-room, the three men, in indescribable pyjamas (the Californian sartorial touch had got to Saladino pretty soon, relieving him of his lounging kaftans and turning him into a kind of majestic fruit tree), gathered round to comfort Diana. Mabel's hair was like a shaggy punk's and covered in coloured coxcombs.

'That's Guille and Rafa's doing,' explained Ignacio, pointing to the dog. 'A friend of theirs has opened a salon on the Strip and has started by practising on Mabel.'

The TV and videos were still going full blast.

'We record everything,' Rafa explained to Diana, 'absolutely everything. Every morning we look at the material and choose what we consider personal documents. Interviews with politicians, actors, etcetera. We're especially interested in people

125

whose astrological charts we have. We keep any interviews which refer to plans, contracts, etcetera. What with our files and our talent, we can guess what will happen to them.'

'And that keeps you amused?'

'Not only that, darling,' smiled Guille. 'We send people their forecast in the post and ask for five dollars cash on delivery. Most of them send us a cheque. I'm not saying it's a lot, but you'd be surprised how many people in California worry about the future. Especially since the Charles Manson business.'

'It's enough for the housekeeping,' said Rafa. 'In fact, we don't spend a lot. It's much cheaper here than in New York. And we buy in La Brea Circus, a funny kind of store where slightly damaged goods end up. Cases of French wine with bottles missing, tins of Iranian caviare with dents in.'

'Ah,' said Diana admiringly, 'I'd like to go. I know this recipe with spaghetti and caviare. So far I've only ever made it with substitutes.'

'Quit those housewifely tips, will you? We have to devise a plan,' Ignacio interrupted.

'That's right, a plan,' seconded Diana, glad someone was taking the reins.

'Diana must keep up her work with Julio. She must use the book as an excuse to follow him as closely as possible and find out which of his entourage may be mixed up in the plot. If she keeps on acting like the village idiot, they won't suspect.'

'What d'you mean by that?' Diana was indignant.

'Nothing. I was talking about your great ability to simulate.'

'Ah, OK.'

'The baddies must think you've swallowed the bait. Meanwhile, we'll protect you.'

'How?'

'Well, um . . . We'll think of something. Don't worry, Encarnita. I don't know what they want, but we have to remember that Julio Iglesias is a target of envy and resentment for many mediocrities simply because he's an international star. They may be trying to use you to eliminate him.'

'Good God!' gasped Diana Dial.

'It's a hypothesis. Anyway, whatever they want, our duty is to be on the alert, protect Julio, and make sure one day Clavé Hair Restorer is used in every corner of the globe. People have to learn there is a quick, definitive and painless way of not only stopping hair falling out but also making top-quality new hair grow more abundantly than ever.'

'D'you think they've had the bottle in their possession long enough to steal the formula?'

'It's possible. Especially, since *you* told that friend of yours what was in the bottle and who it was for.'

Diana hung her head in shame.

'Don't treat her like that,' butted in Guille. 'She's a good soul.'

'What's done is done,' said Rafa. 'It could've happened to anybody. Even us, who look into the future.'

'That's what I was coming to,' interrupted Clavé. 'The future.'

He signalled to Guille and he went into the study. He came back with a big roll of paper, which Ignacio took reverently from him.

'This has to be done perfectly. We can't afford any more mistakes.'

He unrolled a kind of pale-blue map on the floor.

'How lovely,' enthused Diana. 'Is it Venus?'

'Don't be silly.' Saladino cut her short. 'It's the House of Travel.'

'Are we going somewhere?' she hoped.

'It's Julio Iglesias's astrological chart, from the invaluable files of our friends here. We need to know when he's leaving Los Angeles and where he's going.'

'I can ask his press agent for his tour itinerary.'

'Oh, woman of little faith,' snapped Saladino. 'When will you believe in the accuracy of the stars?'

Diana's only faith in that direction was that your eyelashes grow bushy if you cut them at full moon.

'Let's see,' said Ignacio, as he got down on his knees. 'Uranus is in the Eleventh House.'

'A bit to the side,' said Rafa.

'And Jupiter is coming out of the First,' added Guille.

There was a tense silence. Finally, Ignacio raised his face, looked each one of them up and down, and declared:

'His shows in Los Angeles end on the 6th, that is, tomorrow, but he only starts again on the 8th, in Milwaukee, Detroit, Philadelphia, Boston, Montreal, Toronto, Ottawa, Saratoga, Cleveland, Pittsburgh, Chicago, Minneapolis, Jones Beach, Baltimore, the Catskills, New York, and Atlantic City.'

'How extraordinary!' howled Diana, admiringly.

'It's nothing.' Ignacio was obviously as proud as a peacock.

'He always was the best. Even in Gerona he'd take our breath away.'

'There's more,' Clavé went on. 'Damn!'

They all crowded round him.

'Julio Iglesias will spend the day between his Los Angeles and Milwaukee shows in Miami, where he has to do a few personal things and appear at the OIT Festival.'

Clavé had gone pale.

'Here,' he tapped a point on the chart with his forefinger, 'he's in grave danger.'

'Ohhhhhhhhhhh!'

Naturally it was Diana.

The three astrologers rushed to the bookshelves and came back carrying several ancient volumes. Sitting on the floor, they began leafing anxiously through them.

'I've got it!' exclaimed Rafa. 'Adding the breadth of Saturn's aura with the thickness of its influence and subtracting Mars' anaemia, we get the exact number.'

'What is it?' they all cried together.

'The seventh! Julio Iglesias's life is in grave danger on the seventh! Mortal danger, I'd say.'

They were dumbfounded.

'Just a minute!' said Diana, after a while. 'The OIT Festival is in Miami on the night of the seventh. I know because Tender Titi told me; that hairy hound El Puma has been invited to appear. As you know, he's his favourite singer.'

'So it's pretty clear we have to protect him on that night and . . .' Ignacio broke off. 'Quick, get me El Puma's chart.'

'It's only half finished,' apologized Guille.

'Doesn't matter. Bring me what you've got.'

There followed an hour of deliberation, from which Diana was totally excluded. Finally, Ignacio Clavé spoke:

'I think that's pretty clear, isn't it?'

The others agreed.

'Although his chart is completely different,' he explained, 'El Puma will also have problems, smaller ones, on the seventh of this month. That means the danger will be at the OIT Festival.'

'What can we do?' asked Diana.

'Go to Miami. Pack your things. You'll leave first. We don't want to be seen together. We'll get in touch with you in the usual way. An advert in the show-biz pages of the *Miami Herald*, a day before the Festival. Remember, one day before.'

There was a plane to Miami that same morning. Diana still hadn't been to bed, but she didn't care. She Had A Mission.

'Where shall I stay?'

'Best thing is a hotel,' said Ignacio. 'You won't be noticed there.'

Guille reserved the plane ticket and a room in the Everglades for her. 'It's the most chic.'

Diana clapped, and saw herself in her Woman of the World role again.

They spent the rest of the time before the plane left discussing what Diana was to do when she got to Miami.

'Be careful,' said Ignacio. 'If the baddies find you, your life won't be worth a dime.'

'Don't worry. You'll be proud,' she whimpered, 'I'll make you forget we nearly lost everything because of me.'

'Come on, now. I'm sure you'll do very well,' said Ignacio, encouragingly.

'Just one thing,' begged Diana.

'What is it?'

'What sign is Julio?'

'Libra, of course.'

'What are his main characteristics?'

'Sensitivity, imagination, vitality and stubborness. He's

afraid of planes and of making a fool of himself, and he likes grilled steak and Spanish omelettes.'

'Favourite colour?'

'Navy blue.'

'I knew it,' said Diana Dial, 'the ideal sign for a Leo like me. I won't let them take him away from me.'

Chuchuchuca

★ ★

The house of Titi's friend, where he was waiting for Moncho, was
in a neighbourhood known as Little Havana. It wasn't exactly a
house, more a kind of cement shack with a corrugated-iron roof,
divided into two rooms by a garish curtain. One of the rooms had
two beds for Ramiro, the owners, and his daughter. The other
was the kitchen/dining-room with a table, four chairs and a huge
television whose aerial took up half the available space.

Titi opened the door to him.

'You took long enough,' he said, reproachfully.

'The plane was late arriving,' apologized Moncho, 'and then,
that Amancio made me wait bloody ages.'

'If you'd taken the same plane as me, we'd have saved time,'
insisted Titi.

'It's not my fault. I was the one who had to get the information
from Luscious Maria and you know she takes her time.'

They sat at the table.

'Is your friend here?'

'No, he's taken his daughter to rehearsals. Anyway, tell me
how you got on.'

Moncho recounted the conversation with Amancio Escalario.

'That doesn't seem too bad,' murmured Titi. 'A gentleman's
agreement. That's how things work in America.'

'That's what I think. Hey, don't you have anything to drink?'

Titi went to the kitchen and came back with a bottle of Cuban rum and two glasses.

'Now we just have to wait,' said Titi. 'Julio's arriving tomorrow. I bet he uses the hair restorer when he sings in the OIT Festival. He knows El Puma's in the show too, and he can't stand the sight of his flowing locks.'

'I hope you're right. If this doesn't work, it's back to whoring in Chinatown for me.'

'Don't even think about it. Everything's under control, Moncho.' He stroked his hand on the table. 'Trust me.'

Moncho shrugged. Sometimes he thought his lover wasn't pushy enough.

The street door opened and two people came in. A middle-aged black man, and a strikingly beautiful girl, who was probably very young but seemed older because of the layers of make-up. Her platinum-blonde hair, in a mass of violent curls, contrasted with her dusky complexion and very black eyes ringed in turquoise eye-shadow. Her mouth was like a advert for ketchup. Big tits, willowy waist and heart-shaped hips. She wore a cyclamen miniskirt and bolero, silver stiletto heels, and her ear-rings could have provided Christmas decorations for several families.

'How are you?' asked Titi.

'We've a lot to celebrate, son,' said the man, to Titi. 'Didn't I tell you my precious child would be a success? We've got the organizer to include her in the Festival finale. She'll show them that next to her, Charitín is just a ragbag.'

He looked at Moncho. 'So this is your friend.'

'Yes, this is Moncho. Don't worry about us, we'll only be here a couple of days.'

'Please don't insult me by refusing my hospitality. Besides, I'll be very pleased if you'll come to my beloved child's big day, and report the event for your important magazine *Rumour*.'

Tender Titi had got the contact through the magazine's Latin American distributor, and he'd arrived announcing he'd come to report on the Miami Hispanic Music Festival. He'd presented Moncho (who he said was following on in a couple of days) as his photographer, taking advantage of the fact that he had a compact camera.

'So you're all here now,' rejoiced the Cuban. 'Chuchuchuca will be delighted with her father's friends.'

Chuchuchuca smiled and passed her tongue over the ketchup in a libidinous gesture clearly meant for Moncho, and which Tender Titi preferred not to see.

'When's Julio arriving?' asked Titi, coming straight to the point.

'From what I hear at rehearsals, I think he'll arrive the same day as the show, the day after tomorrow in the afternoon.'

Moncho looked at Titi. 'Our enterprise is hanging by a thread.'

'Sssshhh,' Titi silenced him. 'Trust me.'

'A drop of rum?' offered Ramiro. 'I shouldn't drink; as a member of the Church of the Latter-Day Thursday, I'm not allowed, but the Lord Jesus will forgive me because this poor black fellow has lofty resolutions that I'm sure the Creator will understand, and at the final reckoning they'll count for more than the tiny vices he sometimes can't resist.'

'My father,' interrupted Chuchuchuca proudly, 'has been in Miami for twenty years trying to kill Fidel Castro. He's tried many times, but he has terrible luck. The last time he took a motorboat from Key West, packed with grenades and nine gallant heroes, he had to come back early because he ran out of fuel.'

'It was unspeakable bad luck.'

'Yes, poor thing. Another time he sent him a poisoned papaya, but he's so unlucky the doorman ate it and died a ghastly death.'

'I'll do it one day. The Bishop of my Church says I'm predestined to kill the Anti-Christ. By the way, does Felipe Gonsález really want to buy the Rock of Gibraltar to build a marble palace like Versailles on it? Communists are all the same, you know.'

Moncho yawned. Chuchuchuca yawned, looking languidly at him. Later, after some meat pasty and more rum, they all turned in. A bed was made up for Moncho and Titi in the kitchen.

Moncho had been deep asleep for several hours when someone gently touched his shoulder. He opened his eyes and found Chuchuchuca standing next to his bed, holding a candle, and wearing an aubergine-coloured nightie covering not much.

'I like you a lot,' she murmured. 'We can go to the back patio and you can take some photos of me for the cover of my next record.'

'I'm sorry,' said Moncho, hoarsely, trying not to wake Tender Titi, who was snoring beside him, 'I've haven't got a flash.'

'Well, tomorrow then?' said Chuchuchuca.

'We'll see. Sorry, but I'm very tired. We'll discuss it tomorrow.'

Tender Titi sighed and hugged him. Chuchuchuca looked at them with hatred.

'Seems to me it's more than a flash you're missing.'

She turned and disappeared behind the curtain. Moncho thought he heard muffled sobs.

The plot thickens

★ ★

As Guille had said, the Everglades was a pretty fancy hotel. A big gilt fountain full of goldfish in the lobby promised countless comforts: marble staircase, carpets also in gold, and a flurry of hostesses dressed as princesses. Diana Dial forgot her nagging anxiety for a moment and picked up the Restoration-style phone on her bedside table (the rest of the bedroom matched the telephone) to dial the office of Carlos Iglesias (Superbrother), whose number she'd got before leaving Los Angeles.

'If you want to talk about your book, it's best to contact him. Carlos deals with all that kind of thing,' she'd been told.

On the other end of the line, a sweet feminine Cuban voice informed her that Señor Iglesias was busy. Diana left her number and asked him to contact her as soon as possible. Then she called Viceversa.

'I've a few problems,' she told him, her voice trembling.

'I know,' said Viceversa. 'Clavé phoned me, though he did want to tell me what it's all about. I hope the book's not in danger.'

'Oh, no, I'm the one in trouble. But don't worry boss. I'll do exactly what you'd want me to do.'

'I hope so.' Viceversa paused. 'If . . . if anything happens to you, I'll never forgive myself for having got you into all this. We miss you here.'

Holy Mary, Mother of God. Diana was lost for words.

'Pack it in and come home, if you like,' added Viceversa.

'But you said you want the book.'

'You know what I'm like,' said Viceversa, with unaccustomed tenderness. 'I want the book, but I'd rather you didn't do it if it put you in danger.'

'Don't worry, boss,' she said, with pride. 'I know how to look after myself.'

And she hung up. She didn't know why, but the boss seemed gentle. But she had no time to reflect on it. The phone rang, she picked it up, this time it was Carlos Iglesias's secretary giving her an appointment for that very afternoon. She felt proud of her efficiency but again was at a loss to know what to put on. She decided on a simple linen suit, just the ticket for interviews with Important Brothers.

The ex-breast surgeon's office was at 4500 Biscayne Boulevard, 4th floor. The stairs were being repaired, and the office was a terrible disappointment. She expected to find the kind of grandiose setup Humphrey Bogart had in *Sabrina*, but instead it was a bit shabby. A small waiting-room, with a very young receptionist who didn't look up from the switchboard, a sofa and a table which obviously hadn't won any prizes for design, and lots of posters of Julio and framed gold records on the walls. On the table were copies of *People* and *Billboard*.

She waited. She waited, waited, and waited. At last Carlos Iglesias appeared (Diana recognized him from thousands of photos in magazines), his hand out, a dazzling smile at her and a furious glare at the receptionist.

'Why on earth didn't you remind me!' he roared.

'But you told me . . . ' began the girl.   'I didn't tell you anything!'

'Yes, sir,' she mumbled, and bent over the switchboard again.

Carlos broadened his smile even further. 'This way – please follow me.'

And he led her down a narrow corridor, which seemed even narrower because four typists were typing away in it, one behind another.

'These are my colleagues,' he smiled genially.

Diana recognized Silvia, Alfredo Fraile's secretary, who smiled at her sideways without stopping typing.

Carlo ushered her into quite a large, well-furnished room.

'Well? What can I do for you?'

'I was told that you . . . '

'Ah, the book!' He shook his head, as if seized by a sudden sadness. 'That's impossible . . . What did you say your name was?'

'Diana Dial, at your service.'

'The book's impossible, Diana.' He reached for a thick notebook on his desk. 'If I told you . . . '

His face wrinkled in a deep frown, and he tugged his hair over his wide forehead. Diana had to admit he was nicer looking than his brother, and under his sky-blue Lacoste he sported a lovely pair of pectorals.

'If I told you,' he went on, 'the number of publishers who are after Julio to publish books about him. Paying fortunes,' he added. 'Doubleday, to mention just one. You know, the list that Jackie Onassis runs.'

'Oh!'

'And Julio refuses. He doesn't want anyone intruding in his private life. He doesn't want a writer at his side all day, watching whether he has orange juice for breakfast or not, revealing all his secrets.'

'But I want to write a wonderful book, one which reflects my long and enduring admiration for the most extraordinary singer of all time.'

'I know, I know, Diana. But it's impossible. However much I might like it. If it was up to me, I'd say yes now. I know all the details of the tours, the business deals, the records.'

'Well, tell me,' said Diana, very sensibly.

'No, no. Julio wouldn't tolerate it. It's Julio who takes all the decisions, do you see? He's a fiend, he's in control, of recording sessions, tours, absolutely everything. He doesn't sleep, thinking about his career.'

'Poor thing.' Diana understood her hero, but at the same time she couldn't admit defeat.

'Just imagine, sometimes he wakes Ramón Arcusa in the middle of the night because he wants to change some arrangement or other, and everyone has to rush down to the recording studios.'

The idol who never sleeps! *Please God*, thought Diana, *don't let him end up like Judy Garland.*

'Julio's not the type for biographies. He doesn't like intrusion. Even the book Tico Medina wrote about him, with his permission – I think it was called *Between Heaven and Hell* – he even had problems with that, because either Tico wrote something he hadn't authorized, or Julio regretted having told him. Anyway, when the biography was published, my brother spent several months rubbishing it wherever he went and telling people not to buy it.'

He paused and smiled. 'It'd be a pity if the same happened to yours. It'd be a shame, now that we're friends, if a book you published ruined that friendship.'

Diana trembled. First, because Carlos Iglesias's voice had sounded slightly menacing. And secondly, because she didn't want To Cheat Viceversa.

Superbrother got up, bringing the interview to an end.

'Believe me, I'd like to help you, but I can't. Try talking to Julio.' He shrugged his shoulders. 'He may have a brainstorm and agree.'

He led her back down the corridor where the four girls were typing away like maniacs.

'Come here,' he said when they reached Reception, 'I want to show you something.'

He ushered her into a small room full of computers.

'We organize everything from here. These programs record the letters my brother gets from admirers in all corners of the world, asking for photos, autographs, underclothes . . . you know the kind of thing.'

'It's fantastic,' marvelled the journalist.

'We answer them all, we try to please every one of his fans,' he smiled. 'Each request answered means another record sold.'

Such organization, thought Diana.

'There's just one more thing,' exclaimed Diana, remembering the hair restorer. 'I've a serious warning for your brother.'

Carlos looked at her, unable to hide his boredom.

'I've told you to contact him. I'm just a simple surgeon, a man who devotes himself to curing others and will go back to medicine because all this (he made an encompassing gesture) isn't my world. Some people even say I'm robbing my own brother.'

Diana consoled him by patting his muscular and succulent forearms.

'People are very unfair.'

'You've said it. Anyway, try talking to Julio and see if he can sort something out.'

On Biscayne Boulevard once again, her spirits in her boots, Diana Dial decided she still musn't lose heart. It was hellishly humid. She waited twenty minutes for a taxi, got in, and directed him to the theatre where the OIT Festival was being held the next day. The driver took her over a series of elevated freeways which seemed to lead to the end of the world. The asphalt overwhelmed the exuberant vegetation which every now and again battled to regain its former splendour.

'New to the city?' asked the driver.

'Quite,' she said laconically. She was sick of cheeky drivers.

'Lots of vice here in Miami.'

Silence on Diana's part.

'And lots of poverty,' added her companion. 'Ever since the *Mariel* Cubans arrived and began screwing things up with delinquency and heroin, the big Latin American investors are going some place else. It's not the same here any more.'

More silence.

'I have to work miracles to make ends meet. For fifty dollars an hour, you can have my taxi for the whole day.'

She might be naïve, but Diana thought it very expensive, so she kept profitably mute. Seeing she was sticking to her guns, he went on whingeing.

'I've got seven children, and don't know how I'll make out.'

139

Now he's going to try to sell me one, thought Diana. But the driver had more modest ambitions.

'D'you mind if we stop at this supermarket and I buy a bottle of wine on your tag? The cheapest, I swear. What else can an overstressed cab driver do when he gets to an overcrowded home but drink, drink himself senseless?'

Softened up, Diana gave in. The driver bought six bottles.

''Scuse the cheek, but they were on offer.'

Diana paid up. It's an ill wind that blows nobody any good, she mused. She'd been inside a Miami supermarket, and she could always make use of that when she had to describe one in one of her future literary masterpieces in *Rumour*.

The man finally dropped her in front of a big stucco-coloured building, with columns like *Gone with the Wind*, and a façade with gilt garlands and pink cherubim.

'How beautiful,' drooled Diana.

'Yes . . . hip; this is where Dale County's great artistic events take place,' commented the taxi driver, who by this time had already uncorked the first bottle.

She paid and got out. He gave her his card.

'If you need me. I'm free night and day.'

She thanked him and went up to the main door. It was locked. A guard who was prowling around nearby told her the stage door was at the back. Once there, she came up against the most formidable security. Her *Rumour* creditials were useless.

'They're rehearsing,' she was told. 'The press is barred.'

She was about to say to hell with the whole damn thing when a voice from inside, one she recognized immediately, called her name. Lucas from Almería! Her first impulse was to flee, but his bloody great mitt passed over one of the guards and clutched her shoulder.

'She can't come in,' said the guard.

'But I can go out,' replied Lucas.

And he appeared beside her.

'You can't imagine how hard it is to get in.'

'I can imagine perfectly,' said Diana, very seriously, because she was fed up meeting obstacles all over the place, and also because the very last thing she wanted at that moment was to set eyes on Such a Perfidious Traitor.

'You look pissed off,' he said.

She didn't answer.

'Let's get a drink.'

He took her to a bar further down the street. Settled in front of a Coke, he gave forth.

'You'll have to get a special pass for the festival, but I don't think they'll give you one. They only allow the local press and the Yankee press in.'

'For a simple Hispanic music festival?' Diana would rather have not talked to him, but she needed information.

'Haven't you heard?' Her face didn't move, so he went on. 'It's a top-notch affair, Ronald Reagan's coming, so's his wife Nancy, and Margaret Thatcher. The festival's in aid of the anti-drugs campaign, and they're scared of terrorist attacks of all kinds, from Castro's mob to hypodermic-needle manufacturers, who are hopping mad. Only the artists' employees can go in. I'm here because they sent me with the sound equipment.'

Diana looked at him suspiciously. Was Lucas implicated in the plot?

'Is he still just as bald?' she asked.

'Who?'

'Julio, who else?'

'Yes, it's getting worse. And he'll have to do something quick, because El Puma's performing at the end of the festival and Julio can't bear the sight of him with that luxuriant mop.'

'But . . . hasn't he started a new treatment lately?'

'Not that I know of. The girlfriend of the day massages his scalp with his usual lotion and puts rollers in to fluff it out for his shows.'

Perhaps he didn't dare try Ignacio's tonic, or perhaps (and the thought cut her to the quick) *he didn't trust something I gave him.*

'So,' said Lucas, interrupting her thoughts, 'if you haven't come to cover the gala benefit, what the hell are you doing in Miami?'

'I *must* see Julio. It's a confidential matter.'

'For the book, eh? You'll be lucky! Julio himself has given orders your pretty face isn't to show up again.'

Diana pondered. She no longer gave a fig about the book. What she had to do was stop Julio using the hair restorer! Who knew what May of the Mountains and her accomplices had put in the bottle.

'It'd only be for a moment. Just time to tell him something of vital importance.'

Lucas drummed his fingers on the table. Then he asked.

'Did you listen to my tapes?'

'Oh, yes! Fascinating,' she lied.

'Some guy, eh? Think your magazine would buy them?'

'Well,' an idea was beginning to take shape in her head, 'it depends.'

'On what?'

'On whether you help me see Julio.'

'Impossible,' said Lucas. He suddenly looked at his watch. 'It's late, where the hell has that chick got to?'

'What chick?'

'Listen, if I take you to Julio, they'll fire me, and that doesn't suit me until the sale of my memoirs is in the bag. Ah, here she is!'

A spectacular blonde, with swaying hips and eyelashes preceding her by almost ten centimetres, entered the bar, turning every male head. She came up to Lucas, put her arms round his neck and began kissing him passionately. The Almerian used several paper napkins to wipe the residue off.

'This is Chuchuchuca, and this is Diana Dial, a Spanish journalist.'

Chuchuchuca opened her eyes wide.

'Got a camera?' When Diana shook her head, she added. 'Pity, and here am I really needing a good portfolio. To show agents, you know. Having a great voice isn't enough.'

Diana thought, *If her voice is anything like her bum, they'd only have to look at her sideways to give her a contract at La Scala.* The idea that had been taking shape talking to Lucas was replaced by another.

142

She looked at Chuchuchuca with an air of someone in the know. 'You remind me of Abbe Lane,' she said.

'Really?' glowed Chuchuchuca.

'And Dolly Parton a bit too.'

'Ah!' She turned to Lucas. 'I told you Charitín is a washout compared to me.'

Meanwhile, Diana had quickly woven her plan. 'Look, Chuchuchuchuchuca . . . '

'Two too many,' the other girl interrupted.

'Two what?'

'Two chu.'

'Sorry. The thing is, I'd planned to buy myself a complete photo kit here in Miami since everything's cheap. And now I think of it, I could take lots of photos for my magazine. My boss adores discovering talent like yours. If a Spanish impresario saw you, he might offer you a contract to appear over there.'

'Oh!' She elbowed Lucas in the ribs. 'What important friends you've got.'

Lucas shrugged. Women!

'The problem is,' Diana went on boldly, 'I can only fit it in before the festival starts. Tomorrow afternoon.'

Chuchuchuca said it didn't matter.

'That's even better, you can take me in my costume for the show. A darling little number, you'll see, fuchsia with gold braid.'

Diana assured her that she'd like nothing better to photograph her like that, and arranged to meet her at 7 o'clock, an hour before the festival began, in a park near the theatre.

Lucas was still watching them, perplexed. 'Are you sure of what you're doing?' he whispered to Diana.

'Think of your memoirs, sweetie,' she smiled at him. 'We could pay you in dollars.'

And she paid the bill and stood up.

'Stay here, stay here. I've got a pile of things to do.'

The claws are out

★ ★

'That skinny bitch. I'm sure she weighs under twenty pounds.'

Maggie Thatcher was striding furiously up and down the lounge of Number 10 Downing Street. Her husband, who was polishing a saucepan with his pinny on, chose to maintain a discreet silence. When Maggie got like this, war could break out.

'And all for a disgusting festival full of smelly Latins.'

'Don't go, dearest,' suggested Mr Thatcher softly. 'You can always say you're busy inspecting the wigs in the House of Lords.'

'I don't know why I put up with you!' La Thatcher glared at him angrily. 'You can't even clean.'

She grabbed the pan from him, breathed on it and rubbed vigorously with the scarf she had round her neck.

'I have to go, because the Reagans have invited me, understand? And a mere hint from the Reagans is an order for me. How the fuck d'you think we won the Falklands?'

'All right, all right, dearest,' soothed her husband, catching the saucepan she'd thrown at his head.

'The problem is, let's see if you can get it in your thick head, that I've nothing to wear. Or rather, I do. I've a cupboard full of tailored suits and blouses with bows at the neck which would make even the Queen green with envy, and a mountain of taffeta evening-gowns I don't even have to wear, they walk on their own.'

'So . . . ?'

'That anaemic wretch! Whatever rag she puts on suits her better than me.'

Mr Thatcher, who had put the pan in the kitchen, hung the pinny on its hook and adopted a sober phlegmatic English-husband attitude, went up to his wife and tapped her gently on the shoulder with the stem of his pipe.

'Ask Lady Di's advice. She . . . arrgghhh . . . '

He couldn't finish his sentence because Maggie had stuffed his pipe down his throat.

'Are you taking the piss?'

She sat down, sulkily, in one of the cretonne wingchairs Dennis upholstered in his spare time.

'I've got it!' She sprang up. 'It's a Latin fiesta, everything will be hot and exuberant, so I must use the weapons I have. My curves, my hips . . . Nancy Reagan, eat your heart out.'

She picked up the phone. 'Give me Covent Garden.'

Her husband stared at her, horrified. She smiled, astutely. Putting her hand over the receiver, she explained.

'I think the dress Agnes Baltsa wears in the last act of *Carmen* will suit me a treat. With a few alterations, that is.'

It's their loss

★ ★

Chuchuchuca found her father, Tender Titi and Moncho in the
exact position she'd left them that morning to go to rehearsal:
sitting round the table, drinking rum. The only difference was
that on the shabby plastic table-cloth were two empty bottles
and one half-empty.

'You're a bunch of lazy bums,' she said as a hello.

Ramiro was the only one to stir. 'We were all sitting here
thinking of you, honey. How did it go?'

She ignored him. She took some cards out of her *décolletage* and
put them on the table, with an ostentatiously pompous gesture.

'Here are your invitations to the show. These passes will get
you backstage. I hope you won't embarrass me.'

Titi and Moncho stood up.

'You're fantastic,' said Moncho. 'I swear I'll fix the flash for the
camera today.'

'No need.' She shook her powerful curls. 'I've got someone to
take the photos. For an international magazine interested in
promoting new talent.'

'What's the news of Julio?'

'He's arriving tomorrow. Just in time to go on stage and sing.
Listen, you'll come in with me, but once you're in, you're on
your own. Don't bother me with silly things, I'll be pretty busy
looking after my *tenue*.'

146

Titi and Moncho picked up their respective invitations and put them in their back trouser pockets.

'Shall we call Amancio?' asked Moncho, who still thought Titi was the brains of the enterprise.

'Not yet,' decided Titi. 'Besides, we'll see him at the festival. That'll be the time to grab him, with the results in hand.'

Chuchuchuca sat seductively next to Moncho.

'Leave me alone,' snapped Macho Man.

'Jesus, what a temper. And I'd thought of making you my agent.'

Tender Titi picked up one of the bottles of rum (an empty one, of course), broke it on the corner of the table and stuck the shattered neck under the girl's nose like a fist.

'If you keep flirting with my boyfriend, I'll fix your face so you can go in for the Disabled Olympics.'

Ramiro felt obliged to intervene.

'Leave the girl alone. She's a little bitch like her mother.' He turned to the girl. 'Shut up, you, you'll ruin everything.'

'I feel used,' she sobbed. 'Who's singing, anyway? Who's going to make it big in Las Vegas very soon?'

No one answered.

Chuchuchuca finally ran off to her room to rearrange her eyelashes, which had come unstuck.

'Twenty years old and still doesn't know what life's all about,' declared Ramiro. 'It's hard for a single dad bringing up a whore. If only her mother hadn't left me for Ricardo Montablan!'

The others maintained an understanding silence.

Five minutes later, the girl reappeared with everything in place again.

'Know something?' she roared. 'It's your loss.'

She looked straight at Moncho.

Why is Diana unhappy?

★ ★

Diana Dial bought the *Miami Herald* in the hotel lobby and rushed up to her room. Yes, Ignacio's promised advert was there, and she took good note of the phone number she had to ring. But her curiosity (A Woman After All) made her spend a good while reading the female advice column on the opposite page, entitled 'How to Shine on Every Occasion'. Some of the suggestions really gave her food for thought:

> 'MIAMI IS A CITY OF CONSTANT COMPETITION AND INTENSE RIVALRY. THERE ARE MOMENTS IN LIFE, HOWEVER, WHICH BELONG TO OTHER PEOPLE. I REFER TO THE TIMES OTHERS HAVE TO SHINE OR STAND OUT. THINGS LIKE BIRTHDAY PARTIES, GRADUATION CEREMONIES, CONCERTS, HOUSEWARMINGS, ETC., WHERE ONE IS, DAMN IT, JUST ANOTHER GUEST OR SPECTATOR.'

Diana sighed. Patricia Duarte, the author of the article, went on to say, however, that even on occasions when you are not the centre of attention, you can seize the advantage. She gave examples.

> 'IF YOU'RE INVITED TO A DEBUTANTE'S PARTY AND YOU ARE A MATURE WOMAN, DON'T FOOL YOURSELF,

YOU CAN'T COMPETE WITH A BUNCH OF NAÏVE AND REFRESHINGLY BEAUTIFUL YOUNG THINGS. BUT DON'T PANIC EITHER. COME IN SMOKING WITH A CIGARETTE HOLDER, WRAPPED IN FEATHER BOAS, SHEATHED IN SOMETHING VERY ADULT AND REVEAL-ING, SOMETHING NONE OF *THEM* WOULD DARE WEAR.

IF YOU'RE INVITED TO A WEDDING, IT'S IMPORTANT TO UNDERSTAND BEFOREHAND THAT THE BRIDE HAS ENORMOUS ADVANTAGES OVER YOU. SHE COMES IN LOADED WITH FLOWERS, TIARA, VEIL, TRAIN, AND ORGAN MUSIC. BUT THOUGH YOU WILL NEVER COM-PLETELY OUTDO HER, YOU CAN UPSTAGE HER A BIT BY WEARING RED SEQUINS.'

What a brilliant woman, thought Diana, admiringly. She read on.

'IF YOU'RE INVITED TO A CHRISTENING, YOU KNOW THAT BABIES IN EMBROIDERED GOWNS ARE AS HARD TO OVERSHADOW AS RADIANT BRIDES, EXCEPT PER-HAPS BY EXOTIC ANIMALS. GET YOURSELF A LEOPARD, A CHIMPANZEE OR A PARROT, AND TAKE IT TO THE CHRISTENING.

IF YOU HAVE TO VISIT A SICK PERSON IN HOSPITAL, UPSTAGE THEM TOO! WHEN THE ROOM IS FULL OF VISITORS, RECITE A LIST OF YOUR OWN ACHES AND PAINS, REAL OR INVENTED.'

Patricia Duarte could probably do something for Diana's strange feeling in the pit of her stomach. Everything was ready for the final showdown, but she was as miserable as a Sioux who's had his blanket stolen.

'Why was she feeling so uneasy? She thought of Viceversa, his rather absentminded protection, but always there in Times of Crises. She thought of the Basque, and her eyes misted up, but he belonged to that breed of men who just made a girl lose control. She thought of May of the Mountains, in her treachery, whatever it was. In her big lips, her hoarse laugh, her vulgarity, her way of taking life by the horns. Could it all have been a lie, had she never liked her? Had her friendship, so tender, so unshowy, been A Mere Ruse?

At that moment, with the newspaper folded on her lap, with an urge to talk to Ignacio and tell him the latest news, with all the things there still were to do . . . at that moment, she'd have given anything to forget it all and go to a Hollywood cremation arm in arm with May of the Mountains.

She shook her head and woke from her daydream. You have to be strong, May had taught her that too. So she phoned Clavé and explained her plans to him.

'Perfect,' said Ignacio. 'I'm proud of you.'

After discussing the details, there was a pause.

'Diana?'

'Yes?'

'You seem a bit down.'

'It's nothing,' she lied. 'I'm a bit low, that's all.'

'We're going to eat in a Cuban restaurant. Want to come?'

It was the last thing she fancied.

'No. I'll get some rest. Tomorrow's going to be a hard day.'

But she didn't rest. She phoned the taxi driver with the seven children and asked him to take her round the city.

★ ★

In the taxi, Diana remembered she hadn't had a thing to eat all day. It was getting dark, but the lights of Miami were very different from the ones she had admired so much in Los Angeles. Miami was only lit up in stretches, and between one glowing patch and the next was a murky, evil darkness.

'I want a really good dinner,' said Diana, 'and luxury. I'll invite you.'

The driver promised to take her to the most elegant neighbourhood, to a French restaurant. The *maître d'hôtel* looked at them with the air of someone who's seen it all. Diana was wearing her fanciest cocktail dress and her companion a pair of old jeans and bluish shirt patterned with concentric circles of sweat. They waited at the cocktail bar.

'Before we go in, I want to get something clear,' said Diana taking her first sip. 'I don't want you to tell me your life story, I don't want you to talk, except if I ask you to, and I don't want you to offer to take me to any of the dens of iniquity I'm sure you think I'm dying to know. I just want you to keep my company, listen if I feel like talking, and when I'm so drunk I can't stand up, pick me up and take me back to the hotel. And in case you get any perverted ideas, I must warn you that before leaving I gave your name and number to the manager of the Everglades.'

The driver looked at her, mouth open.

'So don't try to rob me, or kidnap me for the white slave trade. I've only got credit cards on me, and I've also left a letter in the hotel asking them to cancel them if I'm not back by tomorrow morning.'

She ordered a second cocktail and downed it in one.

'I want to driiiink. Until ten minutes ago I didn't drink. You're looking at a faithful old example of abstinence and virtue. I could have married a Mormon,' she added. 'But that's all in the past.'

The taxi driver moved his head in commiseration.

'Don't look at me like that. I'm not paying you to look at me, nor to understand me, nor to stop understanding me. I'm paying you to listen.'

She burped, and just then the *maître* summoned them to their table. He lead them to a little illuminated garden where an accordion player was trying not to let 'La Vie En Rose' go green. The menu was short, but intense.

'Soupe à l'Oignon, Escargots Fines Herbes, Boeuf Bourgignon, Filet Mignon, and Sôle Meunière,' announced the *maître*, like someone listing Nobel prizewinners. 'And pâtés, of course. All kinds of pâtés.'

'I'm not hungry,' said Diana. 'But bring this gentleman whatever he wants.'

'Won't Madame drink something?'

'Wine. Lots of wine. The very best.'

'I don't get you,' muttered the driver timidly. 'First you tell me you want a really good dinner, I bring you to the smartest restaurant in the city, and now . . .'

'Look, young man,' Diana interrupted, putting her hand over his, 'Don't try to understand. It's all incomprehensible. I'm a mere shadow of the woman I used to be. This trip was my life's dream: see the world at last, break out of *Rumour*'s four walls, be entrusted with a mission by Viceversa, penetrate the most inner secrets of the man whose every LP I collected. . . . Well, my dear friend, you can stuff it.'

She was talking to herself, as she downed glass after glass.

'All I've done so far is meet guys who want to grope me, or fuck me up – literally,' she added emphatically. 'People who deceive me one way or another and abandon me.'

She was on the verge of tears.

'And worst of all, now I don't know *what* I want.'

She took the cab-driver's hand again.

'This is just a temporary licence, don't get any ideas,' she said. 'What did you say your name was?'

'Remember my card: William Sánchez.'

'You'll be Billy for me, Billy from Miami.' She kept her hand on his. 'But that doesn't give you the right to get fresh, or rape me. Know something? Everything's much easier in my city. It's in a country nobody's even heard of here, I've realized that these last few days. Spain? Ah, yes, next to Chile! Or in Argentina, or Panama. Nobody's here knows where Spain is.'

She stared at the bottom of her glass, melancholically.

'The Basque knew. So did May. Spain's a place where you can't really be a success like Julio Iglesias. But at the same time, everything's so inoffensive, so very small. Do this,' she let go of Billy's hand and cupped hers, 'and you can hold it all; the country, the people. And you yourself are in the hollow of your hand. It suffocates you, but it comforts you too.'

Billy had polished off an onion soup and an almost rare steak, and she had gone through two whole bottles of burgundy.

'Shall we go?' she suggested, hesitantly. 'This place is getting on my tits.'

They went out. She stumbled, and Billy held her shoulder.

'How are your children?' asked Diana.

'The middle one caught meningitis, but my wife says not to worry, she's pregnant again and it'll be great having another mouth to feed.'

'Well, isn't that fine. Where are you taking me now?'

'We could go for a drive. To clear your head.'

'Are you suggesting I'm drunk?' she complained.

But she went anyway. Billy made her get in beside him, and rolled the window down. The humid, warm, sticky air caressed her face and neck, and turned her hair into a mess of seaweed.

'Where are we going?'

153

'Towards the bay.'

'Oh, yes! I want to see the sea, from a jetty.'

'All the jetties here are private. They belong to the apartment blocks round Biscayne Bay, and their owners don't let just anyone in.'

'I want to go to Indian Creek!'

'Julio Iglesias's house? It's too far. Anyway, you can't even get close. They've got massive security, including frogmen. We stick our nose in, and they'll set the dogs on us.'

Diana was quiet, pensive.

'I want a drink then.'

'That's easier,' agreed Billy. 'I'll take you to Little Havana. But first we're going to Miami Beach.'

They took a huge freeway, which suddenly turned into a bridge over the ocean. They crossed a stretch of dry land. 'This is Belle Isle,' Billy informed her, 'a bit more water, and then terra firma.' He drove down several little alleys pervaded with the smell of the sea and eventually came out on to a ill-lit avenue.

'This is the white cemetery.'

Heavens, thought Diana, *another necrophiliac*. She thought of May of the Mountains.

'We're at the bottom of Collins Avenue. Senior citizens from all over the US come here. From the poorest to the richest. Well, the real millionaires retire to Palm Beach. But they,' he smiled, 'they aren't old. They're privileged folk who live out their years in what used to be their summer homes.'

Diana said nothing.

'Look at the buildings. This is the southern part, the cheap hotels where oldies on the lowest pensions come to wait for death. Then, gradually, doorstep by doorstep, as the house numbers go up, the status goes up, until you get to the private palaces at the other end.'

They parked the car and got out. The street smelt of rotten vegetables and baby milk. From buildings which even in the dark you could see were dilapidated came sounds of televisions, and strident voices.

'Damn you!' a rasping croak was heard clearly. 'I'm going to

154

beat you, Johnny Darret, if it's the last thing I do.'

A hoarse cough replied.

It was very hot, but Diana was shivering. They walked in silence up the street, Billy holding her gently but firmly by the elbow.

'Look around,' he said. 'Dentists are springing up all over, the bastards. It's big business in Miami Beach, making dentures. Though the old people in slums like these,' he gestured to the one they'd just passed, 'have no money to get their teeth fixed. Know what they eat? Baby food.'

'Those little pots? You must be kidding.'

'You should see them in the morning in the supermarket, pushing empty carts with jars of purée jiggling in them. They usually like the meat and veg. It's more filling.'

Diana leant against a wall and threw up.

'D'you feel dizzy?' asked Billy, clairvoyantly.

'It's because you're not giving me anything to drink,' replied Diana, between vomits.

Billy put a hand on her neck while Diana sicked her cocktails up to the last cherry.

'Now we're going to a place I know, this'll blow your mind.'

'Good,' said Diana, hiccoughing, 'somewhere that doesn't remind me of anything.'

They staggered back to the car. Billy was in a better state, but he was no monument to sobriety either. On one corner they knocked over several garbage bins, and some outraged voices rose behind them.

'What they hell are you doing?' A doddery old man emerged from the bins, trying to do up his flies.

Beside him was an old bird of eighty with her tits flapping and a smile from ear to ear.

'Aren't you ashamed?' Billy was furious. 'At your age . . . '

'What's wrong, boy?' asked the old man. 'Or d'you believe those tales about there being no sex in old age too?'

In the car, Diana Dial began sobbing disconsolately.

'Who'll look after me when I'm old?' she sniffed, her nose running. 'I've got no one. No oooonnne!'

She stuck her head out of the window.

'I've only got taxiiii driveeeeers.'

Billy put his right arm round her shoulders.

'I know who Lady Di is, I know how to get rid of black bags under your eyes after a night on the town, I know at what age to operate on a child for phimosis, apricot facemasks hold no secrets for me, and I know how much the Windsors charge for appearing at a party, with or without corgis. But it's not enough! I'm alone, and no one will touch me up when I'm eighty and have tits down to my hips.'

'I shouldn't worry about that. I've got seven children, well, eight soon, and the idea of growing old doesn't exactly thrill either.'

'The worst bloody thing is,' Diana took the hand lying on her shoulder and pulled it towards her enough to wipe her nose on the sleeve, 'that I'm Not Happy Now Either.'

She shook her head. 'Viceversa will look after me. Viceversa's a great man, you know? He's my boss. He's built an empire out of nothing. And he loves me. I know he loves me. It's his witch of a wife who's got him under her thumb. Six foot tall, weighs fifty-two kilos, green eyes and natural blonde hair.'

'Who, Viceversa?'

'No, the witch. Some women don't even need to bewitch a man.'

They drove along in silence for a while. Leaving Miami Beach behind, they reached downtown. Suddenly the air filled with sounds: music, talking, quarrelling, shouting.

'I want a drink,' insisted Diana. 'And vice. A lot of vice.'

After driving down various alleyways with people milling around like in a market, Billy suddenly turned the car down a cul-de-sac, took the key out of the ignition, and fixed the steering wheel with a clamp.

'No damn use,' he commented, 'Round here they'd stick on their backs and carry it off.'

Diana tried to get out by herself, but she got entangled in the door and had to ask for help. Billy patiently put her back in her seat, turned her round, and helped her out limb by limb.

'I admire your practical sense,' said the journalist, sincerely. 'What I don't understand is why you don't use it and buy condoms.'

'My wife is a fervent follower of John Paul II.'

'Enough said. Why doesn't she fuck him then?'

The cul-de-sac led into an unpaved road, dotted with neon signs which made the low buildings look slightly unreal.

'Prepare yourself for what you're going to see.'

'You're pretty smart if you think anything can surprise me by now.'

He took her into an unobtrusive little building with no neon at the door, just a little sign saying: 'Bambi's Mother's Nursery'.

'Hey, I asked for vice.'

'That's what you'll get.'

Inside there was quite loud music. 'From Girl to Woman' by the incomparable Julio Iglesias, no less! A young girl in a striped school tunic smiled at them.

'Anything for the cloakroom?'

They carried on down a narrow passage which led into a large room furnished like a kindergarten: playpens, pushchairs, toys strewn around the floor, Walt Disney characters painted on the walls. A globe of the world served as a lamp in the corner.

A girl appeared, dressed the same as the one in the cloakroom.

'A bottle of whiskey and two glasses,' ordered Billy, as he propelled Diana towards some seats with Pluto and Popeye backs.

The young journalist flopped against one of her childhood heroes, her legs askew.

'Uff, I'm pissed. And to think I could have Begun Drinking ages ago.'

The girl in uniform came back carrying a tray with a baby's bottle and two little glasses on it.

'D'you want to choose yet?'

'We've only come to look,' said Billy. 'The lady doesn't know the ropes.'

Diana gave him a furious look.

'Let the orgy begin, I say. I don't like milk,' she added,

looking hatefully at the baby's bottle.

To her surprise, the thing contained pure ethyl.

'Spill that on the carpet,' murmured Diana, after the first sip, 'and the whole State of Florida Fire Department couldn't stop this becoming the fiery furnace.'

The girl in uniform had disappeared, but came back a few moments later with a row of children holding each others waists as if they were dancing the conga. They were all in uniform too.

'You wanted vice, didn't you?' said Billy. 'Well, any one of these kids can give it to you.'

'What!' shouted Diana Dial, springing to her feet, livid.

'Calm down, don't make a spectacle of yourself.'

'Sorry, sweetie, *they*'re the spectacle.'

'The third one on the right's my son. How the hell d'you think we make it to the end of the month?'

'Shut up!' said Diana, horrified. 'This is a nightmare! This is . . . ! Oh, this is Depravity.'

And she ran out, without giving Billy from Miami time to follow her.

Me, *with a transvestite*

★ ★

Like the heroines of so many films, Diana Dial didn't know whether it was rain or tears blinding her as she ran out into the street.

It was tears.

Like the heroines of so many films, Diana Dial ran, ran, and ran, her heart beating wildly.

At 140 beats a minute.

Like the heroines of so many films, Diana Dial stopped to catch her breath and decide where to go.

She hadn't the remotest idea.

Go back to the Everglades Hotel? Never. Not now she'd discovered the Sordid Side Of Life. Find Ignacio? Never. What did he know (with his star charts and all that humbug) of the cesspool she, Encarna Alférez, had nearly plunged into?

Like the heroines of so many films, she only had one choice: walk through the night, without lamp or lantern, without a future, like a stray dog, like a ship without a captain, as the old song says. Walk until dawn and then, perhaps, throw herself in the Seine like Anastasia, the daughter of the Tsar.

And she walked. Stopping now and again, of course, to have a little drink. A rum here, a whiskey there, a tequila somewhere else. A couple of hours later (and it still wasn't dawn!) Diana Dial was so paralytic that the doctor in *Stagecoach* seemed like the guy playing the cymbals in the Salvation Army band on Broadway and 42nd.

It was about four in the morning when she decided (or rather her body decided for her) to lean against something seemingly solid, a door. But it turned out to be the entrance to a filthy bar blaring out hot Caribbean music, and the hoarsest, most unmistakable voice Diana Dial had ever heard.

'Put the blame on Mame, boy.

Put the blame on Mame . . .'

That was the moment Gilda took off her glove, shook her red hair.

'. . . in the South American way . . .'

Aaaahhh. Diana threw her full fifty-nine kilos into the inside of the bar. There he was. Taking off his glove. With his Barbie-doll wig, and the biceps of a docker. With his tempting breasts, his narrow waist and his long curvy legs. With the unforgettable smile of having, despite everything, Faith in Life.

May of the Mountains was wallowing in the spotlight and at that moment Jesus Christ Superstar himself couldn't have made more of an impression on Diana Dial.

'You're a gorgeous Gilda,' she told him in the dressing-room, as May took off his eyelashes and his character's other accessories. The short black curly hair, the bushy eyebrows, the blackheads on his nose appeared one by one. Then his eyes, now full of shame.

May hid her face in her hands, leaning on the basin which doubled as a dressing-table. Her muscular shoulders shook. She was crying. Diana Dial hugged her. She buried her face in May's hair. Suddenly, they both raised their faces and looked at each other in the mirror. They were hideous, but they didn't care. They were too overcome by the miracle of gazing at each other, and seeing Diana take May's face between her hands and put her lips on hers, and kiss them, yes, kiss them, with a passion which, frankly, She Never Believed She Had.

'I've behaved like a shit to you,' said May.

Diana said nothing. She squeezed her tongue between her lips and tried to swallow it down to her heart.

The dressing-room was narrow and uncomfy, but they didn't care. The carpet was covered in stains, cigarette burns and all sorts of ancient guck that had survived those who'd used the dressing-room before them and would survive them too. Neither May nor Diana noticed. Clean or dirty, sweet- or foul-smelling, the floor welcomed them, rocked them, lulled them.

Under May's protective body, Diana Dial smiled.

'If Viceversa could see me now,' she said, before her friend smothered her in kisses once more.

'Your breasts are my breasts, your prick is my prick,' she said, taking advantage of another pause.

May buried her head in her shoulder and kept moving slowly up and down. Diana was going to say something else, but May whispered in her ear, 'Hey, we'll talk later.'

And so it was that Diana Dial, in a bar in Miami, Florida, with a whacking great transvestite inside her, felt a herd of thoroughbreds gallop up her spine to her neck, as the kernel of her body nearest to May of the Mountains burst out in coloured crystals.

'We have to stop Julio using the hair restorer,' said May immediately afterwards, 'or something terrible will happen and he'll blame you.'

'For God's sake, May,' murmured Diana, coyly. 'Couldn't you be more romantic?'

Making up for lost time

★ ★

'I'll never forgive myself for having hurt you,' replied May, for the nth time.

They were in the transvestite's rented room. It had been light for quite some time. The room was pretty squalid but the posters of Marilyn Monroe and Richard Gere were in their usual place over the bed and this detail, added to the mess and smell of perfume and make-up, made Diana Dial feel quite at home. Lying on May's protruding torso, snug between the silicone, she relaxed with her eyes closed and a pleat of pleasure in the corner of her lips.

'It was like a game. And anyway, I couldn't refuse Luscious Maria anything, she'd been like a mother to me when I was on my uppers in Barcelona.'

She kissed her eyelids gently.

'All I had to do was lose the bottle for a couple of days and give it to Enrico. That friend of mine who fixes corpses, remember. He's a friend of Maria's too, he worked for her as a rent boy for years. He got instructions from her, but I didn't want to know what they were. The better I knew you, the more I regretted getting involved in this business. Now I wish I'd been nosier. It'd be useful to know what they want.'

'Ignacio thinks they want to get at Julio through me.'

'That's pretty obvious, darling. The question is why, and who for? And, most important of all, what the hell did Enrico put in that blessed little bottle. What an idiot I am,' he exclaimed, naked in the middle of the room. 'I'll phone him.'

She put a robe on and rushed out.

Diana moved her body into the warm hollow May had just left in the bed. She didn't want to think. Since they'd met up again, Diana Dial had done nothing but feel. Her, Feeling! None of this had anything to do with the stuff she wrote for *Rumour*. It had nothing to do with anything at all; this feeling of belonging, of having a place reserved specially for her at last, a land to reign over.

Unfortunately, it had also nothing to do with Julio Iglesias's songs either, and that to her was heresy. Was her feeling for May of the Mountains closer to the content of the Basque's favourite songs? Luckily, May came back just then, shaking her out of her Important Thoughts.

'That's that,' she cried, overjoyed. 'Enrico doesn't have the slightest idea who's involved in the plot either, but he says he put a dangerous substance in the bottle which makes hair fall out and that it's something to do with El Puma.'

'El Puma!' roared Diana, jumping to her feet. 'That savage!'

'Do you mind,' said May, getting into bed, 'when he sings "Boomerang" and gyrates his hips it really turns me on.'

Diana thought that one day she'd have to make May choose between *them* or *her*, but a certain female cunning learned over the years made her keep quiet for the time being.

'So El Puma is behind it all.'

'I can't say for sure,' murmured May, sticking her tongue in Diana's ear, 'but that's what Enrico thinks. In any case, we have to stop Julio using the hair restorer. God knows what he'll look like.'

Diana didn't even want to think about it. There were several hours before her date with Chuchuchuca in the park. She'd told May and he'd said, 'I'll come with you. I feel responsible, I won't leave you alone again.'

She let her friend lick her and then, with recently acquired confidence, she licked him too. *The ways of the Lord are strange and wonderful*, she thought.

'May.'

'What?'

'D'you think we have a future?'

May hugged her tight and looked into her eyes. 'I swear I'll never have an operation.'

Diana smiled and delivered herself up to a Sea of Sensations once again.

Anxiety in the star's camp

★ ★

'I've never seen him so depressed,' commented the cook.

'Holy Mother!' exclaimed the housekeeper.

'The worst of it is he never wants to talk about it. That's how he is. He never lets it out.'

'Upstairs they say it's because he has to face El Puma,' whispered the housekeeper.

'Bah, rubbish. El Puma's not a patch on the master singing.'

'That's true,' said the cook, 'but it's because of the hair. He goes crazy when he sees the Venezuelan, who doesn't even have to put spray on.'

'But our boy has a wonderful physique. Not an ounce of fat. El Puma, on the other hand, is always on a diet.'

The two woman finished tidying the huge kitchen of the lordly residence at Indian Creek.

'Apparently he's used everything, but nothing works. And he refuses to have a transplant.'

'On principle, of course,' said the housekeeper. 'The master couldn't bear a single hair that wasn't his.'

'And who knows what hair they give you anyway,' commented the cook. 'Nuns' hair, corpses' hair — same thing anyway.'

She made the sign of the cross.

'He's really suffering,' she added. 'And it's only for a charity benefit.'

'He's such a good person . . . He accepts invitations to these festivals, and this is what happens.'

'Are you taking his food up, or shall I?'

'It's all right, I'll go. Though he'll throw it back at me, I bet. He's locked himself in, and keeps watching Yul Brynner videos.'

'Poor thing . . . It's to get himself used to the idea.'

All systems go

★ ★

Ignacio Clavé shot an inquisitive glance at May of the Mountains.

'How can we be sure you're not lying now?'

May said nothing, resigned, but Diana Dial leapt to her defence.

'She had no reason to get involved in this again. Can't you see? She's doing it for me. Because, well . . . ahem, we're very good friends.'

Rafa and Guille started discussing the matter, while Clavé kept his enquiring pupils fixed on the transvestite.

'I'd swear she's a good sort,' said Guille.

'Shame we haven't time to do her chart.'

'I'm a Pisces,' said May, helpfully. 'With Scorpio ascending.'

'Ooooohhh,' they all shouted, except Diana.

'What does that mean?' she said.

'She has a very artistic side, but at the same time she's very insecure, and then she's got another practical side, though a bit crude,' informed Clavé, and went on, 'Neptune makes her indecisive but Mars gives her oomph.'

'Lucky in love?' asked May.

'Neither one thing or the other. Although getting better all the time.'

May and Diana looked at each other, enraptured, and held hands under the table.

They were in a cafeteria in Coral Gables, with only an hour to go before Diana's meeting with Chuchuchuca in the park. Everyone was a bit agitated.

Just as Diana Dial (newly alcoholic, as we know) was raising her second daiquiri to her lips, Ignacio Clavé looked at his watch and dropped the bombshell.

'If Iberia hasn't done the dirty on us again, in five minutes through this door will walk Luis Brunet, our beloved boss, also known as Viceversa.'

Diana Dial choked on her drink.

'My boss!' she yelled, flushed.

'In person,' confirmed Ignacio. 'He phoned me to say he was flying to Miami urgently. And told me some story or other which, to tell the truth, I didn't understand. Something about you, Las Vegas and his lady wife.'

'Oh, no!'

May patted Diana gently on the back to help her spit out the bits of the glass she'd just chewed in her panic.

'I don't believe it!' Diana Dial clutched Ignacio with both hands. 'You know the future, is he by any chance coming for me?'

'I've no idea. Ask him yourself. Here he is.'

And in fact, Viceversa was coming into the cafeteria at that very moment. He looked around, spotted them and smiled broadly.

'But, boss, you in Miami!' exclaimed the journalist.

'I always wanted to see California,' he replied. 'I have to talk to you, Diana. Alone.'

'Boss, we can't right now,' Diana anguished. 'Julio Iglesias's happiness depends on what we do in the next few minutes. A fertile career of international hits may be cut short by the slightest slip-up on our part.'

'I don't give a fig about Julio Iglesias,' said Viceversa.

'But, boss, his picture on the cover sells more copies of *Rumour* than anyone else.'

'I don't give a damn about *Rumour*.' And he held out an implacable hand to her.

'But, boss, without *Rumour*, you couldn't buy leopardskin coats for your wife.'

'I don't give a toss about my wife.'

And the boss's hand kept a tight hold on hers.

'Oh!' exclaimed Diana Dial as stylishly as she could.

The naked truth was revealed. Her boss had realized at long last that she was much better than the other woman, though she might seem smaller and plumper and her blonde hair was not altogether natural. Years by his side, loving him in silence, sharing his triumphs and failures, not asking for pay rises so as not to offend him, so many years of self-sacrifice had at last born fruit! She swelled with pride: everything the *Rumour* agony column advised came true.

She looked at Viceversa with languid eyes. 'Boss, d'you realize we're the living proof that women's magazines never lie?'

'Call me Luis. As soon as we've settled the Julio problem, we'll go to Las Vegas and get married, like in *Dynasty*.'

The others, who'd been silent until them, joined in.

'We have to do your horoscope!' shouted Rafa and Guille, in unison.

'I always knew you'd end up being my boss,' said Ignacio, kissing her on both cheeks.

'You motherfucker, you,' said May of the Mountains, enunciating each syllable.

Diana Dial smiled sweetly and put one of the curls in her fringe back in its place.

'Luis, let me introduce May of the Mountains, the person who's done most for me in the last thirty-two years.'

She turned back to May and, without Viceversa seeing, winked at her.

'D'you want the bridesmaid's dress pink or blue?'

Panic in Biscayne Park

★ ★

'So, honey, you know the law of the Miami jungle: never voluntarily give up the spotlight to anyone. You stick in there, and let the distinguished audience see you properly.'

Ramiro's advice resounded inside the Cadillac like one of the Ten Commandments.

'Ay, Papa,' said Chuchuchuca, 'I'm all nervous, not only for my act, but also for the photos.'

'The bloody photos!' complained Moncho. 'I'd be happier if we were going straight to the theatre.'

'You've no consideration for my career,' said the girl, indignantly. 'What's more, I think you envy me because I'm a beautiful young woman.'

'Silly cow,' shouted Titi, 'can't you see I'm the queen? He finds you disgusting, disgusting!'

'Calm down, kids,' butted in Ramiro. 'You're going to ruin the happiest day of my life – apart from the one when I kill Fidel with my own bare hands, that is.'

They stopped in front of a side entrance to Biscayne Park, got out of the car and walked towards the undergrowth.

'I'm meeting her beside the statue of Simón Bolívar,' explained Chuchuchuca.

'Which one, honey?'

'The whole figure.'

'With or without a horse, honey?'

'Without, Papa.'

'With his sword aloft or prudently sheathed?'

'Sheathed, Papa, guiding the destiny of the Americas.'

'Then it's round here.'

Ramiro lead them to the rendezvous spot. It still wasn't quite dusk, but the plants were already dilating with that kind of drunken exuberance which comes over them at night. Mosquitoes, hordes of them, were everywhere. Chuchuchuca smiled as Tender Titi and Moncho scratched their bites fruitfully.

'You'll be covered in lumps tomorrow,' said the girl with obvious delight. 'Luckily Papa and I rubbed ourselves with a foolproof ointment used by Seminole indians in the eighteenth century.'

She gave her father a conspiratorial dig in the ribs. Ramiro looked at his watch.

'She's late. Maybe she got the wrong Bolívar?'

The minutes passed, the silence deepened and the mosquitoes got themselves better and better organized.

'The things you have to do to get out of bloody poverty,' said Moncho, giving Titi a slap which flattened several hundred flies but left his tender friend's right cheek not a pretty sight.

'Shall we go?' suggested Titi, but Chuchuchuca looked daggers at him.

While the group mounted guard on the statue, Diana Dial was leading the expedition to guarantee the safety of Julio Iglesias and demonstrate the qualities of Clavé Hair Restorer. Next to the leader was Viceversa, who gave her a grope whenever they passed under a giant rubber plant, which was pretty often. Behind them came Rafa and Guille with baseball bats, and May of the Mountains followed them, armed with a huge ornamental comb the size of a rake. Ignacio brought up the rear carrying a plastic bag.

'Good thing we sprayed anti-mosquito stuff,' said Rafa.

'Ssshhh,' interrupted Diana. 'According to my information, we're nearly there.'

They stopped in a small clearing full of wild orchids.

'Pity there isn't time to pick you a bunch,' said Viceversa, looking enthusiastically at Diana.

He took a little dictaphone out of his pocket and murmured: 'Remember to send two dozen of the best orchids to Encarna Alférez, alias Diana Dial, Señora Brunet.' Then he put it away, and went back to ogling his assistant and future wife.

Ignacio Clavé spoke: 'I'll creep up to the scene of the action, spy through the undergrowth, and come straight back. Hold my bag, Rafa.'

He reappeared a couple of seconds later, crimson with rage.

'They're there! They're there all right! Like unsuspecting mice sniffing the cheese. And guess who's with your Chuchuwhatshername?' he asked Diana, 'Tender Titi! That damn queer! And the brute who threatened my life and forced the secret of the hair restorer out of me!'

'Heavens!' exclaimed Diana. 'Now I understand everything.'

'Well, I don't,' said Viceversa. 'Someone prepare a report in triplicate and send it to my secretary.'

Diana shut him up with a kiss. 'We'll tell you later, angel.'

She looked at Ignacio.

'It's very simple,' she explained. 'Tender Titi's lifelong passion for El Puma . . . We should never have trusted him.'

'And the brute?' asked Ignacio.

'Must be his boyfriend. I imagine. Is anyone else with them?'

'Yes, some old guy in a *guayabera* who looks like Cesar Romero in his early films.'

'Probably Chuchuchuca's father. Listen, this is what we'll do. . . .'

They all crowded round her. Diana Dial, Sure of Herself at last, gave them their final instructions.

'What's going on . . . ?' The words died in Ramiro's throat. Guille left him *hors de combat* with a blow on the neck, while Diana jumped on Chuchuchuca and stuck a hanky soaked in chloroform in her mouth. Rafa, meanwhile, had no trouble with Tender Titi, in his best imitation of a boa constrictor, he managed to leave him unconscious from almost fatal strangulation. Ignacio saved himself for Moncho.

172

'I'm a scientist,' he shouted, as he plunged a mysterious syringe into his neck, and Moncho crumpled.

'Oooooo!' said Viceversa, who had merely stood and watched. 'What adventures one has when one abandons the peace and quiet of one's office.'

Diana quickly relieved Chuchuchuca of her fuchsia-and-gold-braid outfit and put it on. Ignacio opened his bag, and out of it stepped Mabel holding in her teeth a wig identical to the Miami girl's coiffure. Diana put it on and the dog wagged its tail happily.

'Little Angel,' commented Ignacio. 'She likes you. She thinks you're a dog too.'

'Wow, wow!' enthused Mabel, shaking her mane.

'So sad Julio's isn't as beautiful as that,' sighed Clavé, admiring the prodigious results of his hair restorer.

'There's no time to lose!' urged Diana Dial. 'Search them.'

They threw themselves on their enemies and stripped them of their credentials.

'Five priceless invitations! Or, rather, four and my guest singer card. Shit, we're one short,' said Diana, counting her fingers.

'Don't worry,' butted in Rafa. 'Guille and I will stay in the car, at the door, in case we have to run for it.'

'We've one too many then!' Diana shouted triumphantly.

'Perhaps we can sell it at the door,' suggested Viceversa.

Diana Dial deliberately ignored the capitalist side of her boss and newly acquired fiancé.

'Forwards!' she roared. 'To the festival.'

Her false mane waving in the wind, she was a veritable Amazon. Viceversa and May of the Mountains, who'd watched the whole scene sobbing and clutching a lime tree, smothered her in torrid looks.

173

Tension mounts

★ ★

The great international singer's inner circle were biting their nails.

'I can't perform for the Reagans and Thatcher with a bald patch. It'll be even more noticeable with El Puma singing just before me.'

The group said nothing, unable to find a solution.

'And there's no way I'm putting on a straw hat,' added the star, turning down his secretary's suggestion again.

'My God,' whimpered the press agent, wandering nervously in and out of the dressing-room. 'We need a miracle, dammit.'

'Idiot!' Maggie flicked her train at her husband. 'Can't you see you're treading on it? I want half a metre free round me or I'll call the bodyguard.'

The commissionnaire bent double as the British Prime Minister passed, and someone somewhere played 'God Save the Queen'.

José Luis Rodríguez El Puma was brushing his eyebrows in the mirror.

'I've got to separate them from my fringe,' he insisted.

'Amancio Escalario's outside,' interrupted his valet.

'God, not again!' complained the Venezuelan singer. 'He

hasn't worked for me for a year. Tell him to get lost. I don't want to see him. He's the worst rogue ever.'

Diana Dial couldn't believe it. The man who opened the door, smiling like a saint and dressed like an American musical comedy, was none other than the Basque, who had taught her so much about Customs and Usage.

'I'll get a steady job, Diana. I'll mend my ways. If you like, we'll get married, have children, and call the eldest Julio.'

Diana stuck her nose in the air and walked past him, ignoring the man she'd met in Venice, when She Was Very Different.

Viceversa and Ignacio Clavé (with Mabel hidden in the bag again) followed her. May brought up the rear, crying her heart out.

'But what the hell's the matter?' asked Diana Dial.

'I know I'm going to lose you. I know it!' she sobbed, beating her silicone breasts.

'Don't be silly. You and I are just beginning to learn what makes men tick.'

'We'll be late, as usual,' complained Nancy. 'All because you can't put your false teeth in right.'

The President didn't answer because in fact he'd put his hearing-aid where his denture should be and he couldn't hear her properly.

'Sometimes I think I prefer Bush,' insisted Nancy. 'There's more of him left.'

'How beautiful,' exclaimed the President, as they settled themselves in the VIP box. 'Was Grenada like this little theatre before the invasion?'

'Look at that harpy,' whispered Nancy. 'What on earth has she got on?'

Maggie smiled peevishly and twiddled her castanets.

'There! Cla-cla-cla.'

'Eh?' asked Nancy, embarrassed.

'*Voilà la Carmencita*, as Merimée said,' replied Maggie.

Reagan turned to his bodyguards. 'Have they sung yet?'

'No, Mr President. They were waiting for you to arrive.'

'Ah, how nice of them! Where is Miami?'

'In Florida, Mr President.'

'What did you say?'

'Floridaaaaa!' roared the bodyguards.

'Ssshhh,' warned Thatcher. 'And budge up a bit, I want to put my shawl over the balcony. Huuuuuuulio may dedicate something to me.'

'Eureka!' cried the press agent. 'I think I've got it!'

'Got what?' asked the international idol, sulkily.

'The solution to our problem.'

'*Our* problem? *My* problem, mine and only mine! You've got a whole mass of revolting hair. God always gives inferiors something like that. All right, what is it then?'

'Remember that journalist? The silly twit, the Spanish one, the one who wanted to write a book about you?'

'Yes, I remember her. Too old for me.'

'That time she met you, she gave you something, something for your personal use.'

The international idol thought for a few moments.

'Ah, yes, I'd forgotten!' he exclaimed, at last. 'She said it was a hair restorer.'

'What if it is?' asked the agent, daringly.

'What if it isn't?' asked the singer, sensibly.

'Anyway,' the press agent contemplated his boss's pate, 'you've nothing to lose.'

'I'll fire you and give you bad references to boot,' said the Transatlantic Heart-throb angrily.

'I meant trying it doesn't cost anything.'

'All right. Where is it?'

'I've sent Lucas to fetch it. He won't be long. Luckily, he kept it in the luggage.'

The international idol sat down in a chair.

'Quiet, everybody,' warned the press agent. 'He's relaxing.'

Song of Songs

★ ★

'They're all wearing nylons,' wailed Diana.

She was in a corner backstage, terribly nervous, with May of the Mountains groping her crotch, and Viceversa and Ignacio discussing whether or not to let Mabel out.

'It's the fashion here,' said May. 'They all wear nylons even though they're sweating cobs.'

'How awful,' complained Diana. 'I really miss Barcelona.'

May was about to cry again, but the orchestra struck up a lively tune and a mulatta rushed up to Diana.

'Señorita Chuchuchuca, you're on now.'

'Me?' asked Diana, putting her wig straight.

Ignacio intervened: 'The lady's not quite ready.' And in a voice low enough for only Diana to hear: 'You've got to get to Julio. His dressing-room's on the other side of the corridor, a blue door. We're counting on you. God knows if we'll be in time to avert a catastrophe.'

But the girl pulled Diana towards the stage, and she let herself be carried away by the magic of the moment. The audience, who had already heard singers from all over Latin American plus a certain José Luis Perales elegantly representing Spain, wanted more.

Diana advanced to the centre of a stage decorated with tropical fruits and flowers.

177

The orchestra struck up.

Paralysed, the journalist raised her hand to her throat. She tried to sing something. *Grrr, screeeech, urrrgggh*, were the only sounds that came out, so overcome was she.

She cleared her throat. The orchestra stopped.

'Forgive me,' she said clear as a bell, 'forgive me, ladies and gentlemen, forgive me, distinguished guests.'

She bowed low, like people in *Hello!* when they pay their respects to royalty, then rushed off the stage shouting:

'I have a Mission!'

'What's going on?' asked Nancy Reagan.

'They're just being Latin,' replied Maggie.

The President was asleep.

Diana Dial ran to Julio's dressing-room, brushing aside anyone in her path.

'Stop!' shouted the guards as she approached.

She kept running.

'Stop!' they warned as she reached the door.

She took no notice. There was no stopping her.

She opened the door and there he was! Gazing at his ample forehead in the mirror, with the bottle of Clavé Hair Restorer in his hands!

'No!' roared Diana. 'Never!'

Julio couldn't believe his eyes.

'I say, what's this intrusion in my privacy? This place is sacred.' he muttered.

Without a word, Diana grabbed the bottle from him. Then, holding it a safe distance from her, she ran as if possessed by the spirit of the guy who lit the Olympic flame at the recent Games. As she passed her gang, they were aghast.

'For God's sake, darling,' moaned Mayo. 'Get rid of it!'

'Throw it away, but don't let go,' advised Viceversa.

'We should keep a bit to analyse!' shouted Clavé.

'Woof, woof,' barked Mabel, in solidarity.

But Diana Dial galloped towards the stage. There he was. El Puma, in mid love song. The girl stood before him, her eyes shining with rage, and declared dramatically:

178

'You traitor!' The orchestra stopped playing. 'Trying to upstage my favourite singer!'

And she threw the bottle into the stalls.

After the explosion, when the smoke had cleared, El Puma said, bewildered:

'They're all bald.'

'Where? Where was it?' asked Ronald Reagan. The bodyguards dragged him out together with Nancy and Maggie, both unconscious and bald.

Diana trembling, looked backstage. Her gang were applauding frantically.

'You've saved him!' shouted Viceversa, going up to her and hugging her. 'I'm making you the editor of *Rumour*.'

'I want a job for May of the Mountains,' demanded Diana. 'Now Tender Titi's been fired, it'll be a big help having my friend in the archives.'

'Agreed,' admitted Viceversa. 'Come on, let's go to Las Vegas and get married straight away.'

At that moment, something sublime happened to Diana Dial.

Julio Iglesias came towards her, his arms outstretched.

'Diana! I know the whole story! You've saved me by a hair's breadth!'

'Well, I had a hand in it too,' butted in Ignacio. 'Clavé Hair Restorer at your service. I invented the primitive formula which will combat your baldness once and for all.'

'Wonderful, talk to my manager. And now let me show my gratitude to this young lady. Diana, darling, come with me for a few days to my mansion at Indian Creek.'

Julio's eyes shone with irresistible fascination. Diana took a step towards him. She looked at Viceversa and asked herself whether she could betray the man who'd given her the chance to become A Woman of the World. She looked at May of the Mountains, and the memory of their intimate moments made her feel Really Randy. But there was Julio, offering her a holiday in his Miami house complete with Satellite Dish. And Julio represented everything she wished for.

'Come on, decide,' urged the star.

Diana Dial said nothing. The images of her life whizzed round and round her small but honest brain.

'Leave her alone!' shouted someone suddenly. 'That woman belongs to me!'

It was the Basque. He invaded the group and joined the chorus of suitors awaiting her answer.

Three Men To Choose From, thought Diana, *And a transvestite*, she added deep down. May of the Mountains was a certain part of the deal, whatever she chose.

Diana had a sudden flash of inspiration.

'I want to get married,' she said.

If her poor mother could see her now! There was silence, none of them said anything, as if the police had just arrived saying hands up. The first to speak was the Basque, repeating his previous proposal: have a family, settle down, etc. Nothing Exciting, thought Diana.

'We'll leave for Las Vegas straight away, we'll get married, and then we'll gamble a few pesetas in a casino,' offered Viceversa.

Then Julio spoke:

'I'm prepared to consider the possibility of contracting a second marriage.'

Diana caught her breath. She remembered He and Isabel Preysler had had their liaison annulled.

'In church?' she asked.

'In church,' agreed Julio.

'That's playing dirty,' cried Viceversa.

'I could tell him a thing or two,' remarked May, under her breath.

With vertiginous speed, Diana Dial came to a conclusion. With Julio it could never be.

'No,' she said firmly.

'What d'you mean, no?' asked the singer, taken aback.

'What did she say?' enquired Reagan, waking up, in the car, to his bodyguards.

'She said no.'

'The girl's crazy,' commented the President.

180

'But, why?' said Julio, despairingly.

'Because dreams shouldn't become reality.' She was delighted with Her Conclusion. 'It's better they stay illusions, to light our way.'

'Well said,' crowed Viceversa. 'She's not just a pretty face, you know.'

'I'm going with my boss.'

'Who's Viceversa?' asked the President. His bodyguards explained patiently again as they went up the steps of Reagan's private jet.

'I'm going with the man who makes my dreams possible,' declared Diana. 'Don't be sad, Julio. You've got your hair restorer. Think of me whenever you use it.'

'An angel, a true angel,' sobbed Ronald Reagan, surveying the scene from his window as he flew over Miami.

Viceversa took Diana's hand, and Diana took May's, Ignacio and Mabel took each other's hand, and they all ran towards the door. The Basque and Julio were left alone.

'Up till now I was the positive character in this story, but she has changed everything. D'you have a job for me?' asked the Basque.

'I'll never find another girl like her,' sighed Julio. And he added: 'What a great title for a song.'